# LOVE UNDER TWO WILDCATTERS

*Lusty, Texas 2*

## Cara Covington

**MENAGE EVERLASTING**

Siren Publishing, Inc.
www.SirenPublishing.com

A SIREN PUBLISHING BOOK
IMPRINT: Ménage Everlasting

LOVE UNDER TWO WILDCATTERS
Copyright © 2011 by Cara Covington

ISBN-10: 1-61034-270-4
ISBN-13: 978-1-61034-270-4

First Printing: January 2011

Cover design by *Les Byerley*
All art and logo copyright © 2011 by Siren Publishing, Inc.

**ALL RIGHTS RESERVED:** This literary work may not be reproduced or transmitted in any form or by any means, including electronic or photographic reproduction, in whole or in part, without express written permission.

All characters and events in this book are fictitious. Any resemblance to actual persons living or dead is strictly coincidental.

Printed in the U.S.A.

**PUBLISHER**
Siren Publishing, Inc.
www.SirenPublishing.com

# LOVE UNDER TWO WILDCATTERS

*Lusty, Texas 2*

### CARA COVINGTON
Copyright © 2011

## Prologue

*El Paso, Texas, 1986*

The wind rumbled like a freight train as it tore through the alley above their heads. Or maybe it was like a coyote, a huge and hungry beast, hunting them.

Eleven-year-old Colt Evans tried to push that thought out of his mind. *Doesn't pay to give in to the fear. They only beat you harder when you give in to the fear.*

Better to think about the good things. He had a sturdy piece of cardboard under him, a blanket tented over him. The dumpster beside him, even though it stank, kept off most of the wind and hid them both from the street gangs and the cops.

Best of all, he had Ryder Magee on the other side of him. He and Ryder were best friends. No, they were brothers, blood brothers since last night. He looked over at Ryder now. His brother's black eye was nearly healed. That bruise marked the beginning for them. He'd come upon Ryder a couple of days ago, being beat on by two older bastards—likely teenagers thinking the skinny Ryder made an easy target. Colt had beat them off with a pipe he'd found lying in the alley.

He and Ryder had a lot in common. Colt had lit out from the dive his mother lived in a couple of months ago when her latest boyfriend had used him as a punching bag. His mom had been too stoned to care and likely didn't miss him one bit. Ryder had been in a similar fix, only it wasn't just a punching bag his mom's dealer wanted to use Ryder for. So Ryder had left home, too, the same day Colt had met him.

El Paso began to settle in for the night around them.

"That was good stuff you got for us," Ryder said.

"Yeah, it was all right."

Colt had scored them dinner from a restaurant over on Lee Trevino. The manager there took pity on him and would give him some food every once in a while. Guess it made the man feel all righteous. Colt didn't care about that as long as he had something to eat.

Tonight, at least, they weren't hungry.

"You know all the best places," Ryder said. "I'm going to learn about the best places, too. And we'll find more places, won't we, Colt?"

"You bet. So what do you think of life on the street so far?"

"Sucks, but it's better than what my old lady and her dealer had in store for me."

Beside him, Ryder shivered, and Colt knew it was from more than just the cold.

"Yeah, it sucks. But you know what? Someday we're going to have a real home, a home of our own where no one will tell us what to do or beat on us. And we're going to have lots of money and lots to eat. We'll never be cold again. We'll own our own business, and folks will look up to us and respect us."

"You think we're going to do all that?"

"Bet your ass."

"You figure we might even get married someday?"

Colt shook his head. "Nah. You get married, then you have to live separate. We're brothers for life, no matter what. Remember?"

"Course I remember. But maybe we don't have to. Live separate, that is. Maybe we can marry the same woman. Then we'd be a real family, wouldn't we?"

Colt thought about this some. "Seems to me," he said at last, "that when you're grown up you can do any damn thing you want." At least, that had been his experience so far. "So, yeah. Why the hell not? We'll make that one of our goals."

"Yeah, why the hell not?" Ryder echoed.

Colt hunkered down and pulled the musty blanket Ryder had filched from his place closer around them both. Ryder wasn't as tough as Colt yet, so Colt would watch over him. But he would be, and soon, he bet.

Colt wouldn't think about if his dreams would ever come true. He'd only think about what his life would be like *when* his dreams came true.

His mother was thirty-six. He nodded once, decision made. He and Ryder would have all they dreamed of having by the time they were thirty-six.

Why the hell not?

# Chapter 1

*Present Day*

Colt Evans wandered over to the floor-to-ceiling windows that offered an expansive view of downtown Houston at midday. From high up on the twentieth floor, he could see as much of the city that lay in that direction, stretched toward the gulf to the south. *City as far as the eye can see. Reckon some people would actually enjoy this view.* Houston's particularly flat topography lent itself to spectacular panoramas, more than any city he'd ever been in.

"Now that's just too much town for this Texas boy." His best friend since childhood and partner these last twelve years, Ryder Magee, joined him in his window gazing.

"I was just thinking the same thing," Colt agreed.

"Likely, since the Benedicts called us here, they're fixin' to toss in with us," Ryder said. He kept his voice quiet, and Colt understood the inclination. They were here in the boardroom of Benedict Oil & Minerals, invited guests, and, hopefully, soon-to-be business partners. However, they stood on Benedict turf, not their own, and so, caution seemed prudent.

Colt and Ryder had proven themselves to be no slouches in the corporate arena themselves. They'd formed *Dos Hombres Wildcatters* on the heels of the collapse of *Tres Hombres Wildcatters*, just after Morton Barnes ditched them, taking the balance of their bank account with him. They'd built a solid reputation as Wildcatters who knew where to drill. The company had gone from being only two strays from El Paso with a portable rig behind an old Ford half ton to a corporation with more than two hundred employees and a half dozen drills in operation at any given time.

Of course, over the last couple of years, business had slowed, as it had all over the country. Which made the possibility of going into business with the Benedicts a sweet deal as far as Colt could see. The Benedicts had a history of not only staying afloat during tough times, but prospering. More than a century of business success didn't lie. That was the kind of history Colt could get behind.

The door opened, and both he and Ryder turned to face their hosts.

They'd met both Joshua and Alex Benedict long before they'd ever begun negotiations for this deal. The world of oil and minerals in even as cosmopolitan a city as Houston was a small one. The Benedicts were Texas born and bred, same as he and Ryder. The major difference between them was that, while Benedicts generally came into the world complete with engraved silver spoons, both Colt and Ryder had scrambled in the dust of the streets of El Paso for their living—and before either had even reached the age of twelve.

"Thanks for agreeing to meet with us on such short notice," Joshua Benedict said. He stepped forward, offering his hand. Colt and Ryder moved away from the windows to greet the two men. Both Benedicts had solid handshakes.

Colt thought there was nothing worse than shaking hands with a man whose palm put him in mind of wet noodles.

"Our pleasure." Invited to sit by gesture, Colt took a seat adjacent to the chair Joshua stood behind. Ryder sat next to him, and they waited for the Benedicts to make the next move.

"We've vetted your company and run the proposed contract past our board of directors," Alex said. "The vote was unanimous. Gentlemen, we're in business."

"That's good news," Colt said.

"You won't be disappointed," Ryder added.

"Our legal department will courier copies of the contract back to your legal department this afternoon," Joshua said. Then he looked at his brother. When Alex nodded, he said, "We'd like to discuss another matter with you, if you don't mind. A matter that is both confidential and personal."

Colt had sat in enough business meetings to understand *this* was the real reason they'd been called to meet face to face. He met Ryder's gaze. They'd been best friends long enough that some communication could often be carried out with just a look between them.

"You can rest assured we'll respect your confidence," Ryder said.

"We understand the two of you sometimes still like to go out on a site yourselves and drill," Joshua said. "I overheard you lamenting days spent in the office instead of on the rig."

Colt recalled the party they'd been at where Joshua overheard that comment. Since both Benedicts seemed nervous, Colt smiled, hoping to put them at ease. "No secret there. We're wildcatters down to the bone. Business is good, and we couldn't be happier about that. But we do miss the actual work."

"Matter of fact," Ryder said, "we still have our original rig, and though it looks a sight, it performs better than some of our newer stuff."

"Uncle Carson often moans that most of the newer equipment we buy is junk," Joshua said.

Carson Benedict had retired a couple of years before, turning the company over to his nephews. "I'd say I have to agree with your Uncle Carson," Colt said.

"Is it true that when you started out you drilled as many wells for water as you did oil?" Alex asked.

"When we started out, we took any job we could get," Ryder said. "Drilling for water isn't all that much different than drilling for oil, except you don't usually have to go down as far."

Joshua and Alex again traded a look. Then Alex leaned forward. "We have one more question for you. And I'm afraid it's very personal."

Colt couldn't say he'd actually seen a grown man blush before. To say he was intrigued by this entire conversation would be putting it mildly.

"We've known each other for years, and now, we're going to be business partners," Ryder said. "So ask away."

"At the Carstairs' party, around Christmastime last year, we chatted for a bit, if you'll recall. Then, later, we couldn't help but notice you *both* left with Melissa Simms. Would we be wrong in assuming that the three of you were very pleasantly occupied together for at least the rest of the night?"

Colt fought his own blush. He shot Ryder a quick glance and could see his best friend was in the same boat. "We don't generally kiss and tell, but since we are being all confidential here and everything, then no, you wouldn't be wrong in that assumption."

"Actually," Ryder's voice sounded just a tad strained, "we were all three pleasantly occupied for several days."

Colt didn't know what he expected, but the relieved smiles both Benedicts wore surprised him.

"Are either of you men currently in a relationship?" Joshua asked.

Colt felt his left eyebrow go up. "Haven't been for a while now, no."

The brothers' smiles got even wider. Then Alex sat forward. "In that case, we have a drilling job we'd like you to do for us, as a favor. You'd be drilling for water, not oil. There's just one catch, though."

Colt smiled. "There often is."

\* \* \* \*

*Two days later*

Susan Benedict paused in the act of scraping paint off the trim of her new old house. Using the back of her hand, she wiped the sweat off her forehead then shook her hair. Tiny bits of brown paint flecks floated from her hair to the ground. *I should have worn a hat.* She'd awakened full of energy and decided today was the perfect day to tackle the job of scraping the trim. Anyone who knew her wouldn't be the least surprised she'd neglected to don protection for her hair. Susan tended to hit the ground running, jumping in with both feet. She wasn't a vain woman by any means, and this was never so true as when she was hip deep in a project. How she looked never entered into her thinking.

All that mattered to her at the moment was making this house as beautiful as possible and doing as much of the work on her own as she could.

She considered herself lucky that she'd been raised in a larger than average family, by parents who believed hard work was good for the soul. She'd never been one to think herself better than anyone else just because her family had been blessed with great gobs of money.

She took a moment to gaze around the property, a piece of her heritage that had come into the family sometime in the late eighteen hundreds. This house, vacant for years, had once been the domain of whichever Benedict had decided he wanted to work on this end of the family ranch.

And now, this century-old home, in the middle of nowhere, was becoming *her* home. The isolation here suited her current needs to a T. Alone, at the far corner of Benedict land, she could hunker down and not think about those nasty envy attacks she'd been having lately.

Her best friend finally healed from the trauma of watching her family murdered years before and married her two favorite brothers, and Susan should have only been weeping with joy, not crying in her beer about her own loneliness.

Embarrassment still swamped her when she thought about the way she'd behaved at the wedding reception. Not only had she gotten drunk during the party—something she never did, and thank God her brothers and Kelsey had already left on their honeymoon—but then she'd blubbered all over her other brothers' shoulders.

Susan had believed herself resigned to the fact there were no manly men left in the world outside of family and that she would live the rest of her life as a single woman. Apparently, she wasn't as resigned to that fate as she believed. So she'd come out here, determined to keep herself busy and build some kind of life until she got her emotional house in order.

She was a twenty-first century woman, for heaven's sake. She was supposed to be perfectly happy with her business successes and her circle of friends and family. A twenty-first century woman did not need a man, or two or three, to make her life complete.

*So get over yourself and* be *a twenty-first century woman.*

The sound of an engine bracketed by the creak of metal on metal made her turn and look toward the end of the lane. A cloud of dust rose up into the dry September Central Texas air, confirming what her ears had heard. A vehicle had turned off from the state road, heading toward her.

Shielding her eyes from the sun with her left hand, she rested her right on her hip and shook her head at the sight. The dilapidated Ford pickup truck would never see twenty again. Hitched to the back of the vehicle, looking just as rusty and reaching toward the sky, was some sort of metal equipment.

"Well, boy, howdy. What the hell…" Then, recognition of what that piece of equipment was set in, and she realized the vehicle had not turned down her lane by mistake.

Up until this very moment, she'd had the utmost faith in Alex and Joshua's judgment. As the rickety rig headed her way, she didn't know what to think.

She stepped out from under the overhang of her front porch so the driver of the truck could see her. She didn't need a mirror to know what this unseen person would be seeing when she stepped into view. She'd tugged on her oldest pair of blue jeans and donned her rattiest shirt before she'd started scraping the paint off the trim. It didn't make any sense to wear anything but rags when all she'd had on the agenda for the day was being alone with some hard, dirty work.

The truck slowed as it neared, finally coming to a screeching halt about ten feet from where she stood. Two doors swung open at the same time, and a man stepped out of each.

Susan slowly lowered her hand as she looked from one to the other of them. Tall, muscular, one with blond hair, the other with dark hair peeking out from beneath twin battered Stetsons. In a move that seemed choreographed, they each peeled dark sunglasses away from penetrating eyes and gave her the once-over, hot gazes leaving nothing unscorched.

Susan swallowed as her slit released moisture onto her panties and her nipples tightened.

The driver cocked his head to one side, his gaze zeroing in on her traitorous breasts before focusing on her eyes. "Are you the woman who's looking for a couple of really good drillers?"

"You must be Texan." Only Texans, in her estimation, could brag about their sexual prowess and make it sound like innocent conversation.

"Yes, ma'am, just a couple of strays from El Paso looking for a warm, willing woman to take us in." The driver managed to say that with a straight face.

Susan could tussle with the best of them. Having four brothers meant there wasn't much a man—or two—could toss her way that she couldn't handle. "I don't know. I'm seeing a lot of rust, there. I'm thinking the equipment might be past its prime, maybe doesn't even work anymore. I'd be too afraid the intense action of nonstop drilling might prove too much and the bits might break."

"Well, now." The passenger spoke for the first time. Susan could see his dark eyes sparkling from where she stood. "You'll pardon me for saying that sounded like a challenge. If you give us a chance to loosen things up a little and lube them down, we'd be pleased to give you our very best shot."

Susan felt her female parts heat to the point of producing steam. It had been a long time since she'd engaged in this kind of heavy-duty flirting. Damned if she hadn't missed it. She decided to push it just one little bit further. "I don't doubt you'd be pleased, cowboy. Question is, would I be?"

"Darlin', we absolutely guarantee complete and total satisfaction." Being Texan, the driver had no lack of self-esteem.

"We'll see." Would they? Had Susan just committed herself to taking these two men for a ride when she didn't even know their names?

They were tempting, very tempting. Before she could get herself into any more trouble, she took one step forward and held out her hand. "Susan Benedict. Am I to assume my brothers sent you?"

"Colt Evans. This is my partner, Ryder Magee. And yes, Alex and Josh sent us." Colt shook her hand then stood to the side.

Ryder stepped forward, accepted her hand, and completed the introductions. "Ma'am."

"I haven't done anything to cause my brothers to seek revenge, so I'm going to assume you're the real deal and know how to work that thing," Susan said, nodding toward the rusting portable drilling rig in the back of their truck.

"Don't you worry none, we know how to handle our equipment," Ryder said.

She snapped her gaze to him. His angelic expression was really very well done. Beside her, Colt coughed, but she knew the sound of a cutoff laugh when she heard it.

Susan sent Ryder a considering look. "That's what they all say." She shook her head.

Colt stepped forward and reached out toward her hair. She stood perfectly still, her gaze locked with his as she waited to see what he would do.

"I've heard of painted ponies. You're the first painted woman I've ever met, Ms. Benedict." He used a delicate touch to pull a few paint flecks from her shoulder-length blond hair.

"You're the first man to compare me to a pony, Mr. Evans. I'll have to think some before I know how I feel about that."

"Well, now," Ryder stepped closer, "there are some similarities. The very best ponies are lithe and lean and just made to be ridden."

"Once they've been taken in hand and tamed, of course," Colt added.

A twenty-first century woman should be outraged at such talk. Outraged, insulted, and ready to land a couple of well-earned slaps on smug male faces.

Susan sighed as she felt her arousal climb. She guessed it was time she stopped lying to herself.

She might live in the twenty-first century, but her female parts clearly wept for an earlier time, a time of manly men who knew how to be true masters in the saddle.

## Chapter 2

"I'm sorry, Mr. Barnes. The bank cannot, and will not, extend you any more time to catch up the arrears on your mortgage, nor will we extend you any more credit. The deadline stands. You have fourteen days before the bank forecloses."

Morton Barnes narrowed his eyes as he stared at the fat little weasel of a bank manager sitting across from him. The nameplate read Frederick K. Sanders, but Morton had never laid eyes on the man before today. He'd made this appointment, expecting to meet with Earl Jones, the man who'd been manager of this bank for the last twenty years. Jones had been a good old boy, born and bred right here in Houston. Hell, Jones' mama and his own, rest her soul, had sung together in the Methodist church choir.

This Sanders fella looked too young to have been given such a position of authority as manager. Worse, he sounded like a damn Northerner. What was this world coming to?

"You're new here, son." Morton pitched his tone and knew he sounded sincere, if a bit patronizing. He figured the little prick likely wouldn't pick up on the latter. "I reckon you're still a bit wet behind the ears. That's all right. I can understand that. We all have to start out somewhere, after all. But see, my family's been dealing with this bank for longer than you've been alive. My daddy had all his accounts with this bank, and my granddaddy sat on the very first board of directors and was a great personal friend of the bank's founder. So, now you know who I am. It's only fifty thousand dollars I need to borrow, and it's not really a new loan, just an extension onto my mortgage. And I'm not asking for a ridiculous amount of time, either.

I only need a couple of months to set everything to rights. Now, you go on ahead and call whoever it is you have to call to get the okey-dokey, and we'll be in business."

Morton smiled and nodded his approval when Sanders picked up the phone. "Please send in Mr. Gruber."

Morton had never heard of this Gruber person, either. He figured it was a sad damn world when you couldn't even depend on knowing the folks in charge of your money.

The door behind Morton opened, and a man in uniform entered. Morton realized Mr. Gruber was a security guard.

"Yes, sir?" Gruber's voice sounded gravelly, the voice of a man who'd smoked too many packs of cigarettes and likely quaffed too many bottles of Jack.

"Mr. Gruber, would you please escort Mr. Barnes out of my office and out of the bank?"

"Now, see here, Sanders!" Morton surged to his feet, his temper ready to explode. Out of the corner of his eye, he saw Gruber take a small step forward and put his hand on his side arm.

"No, sir, *you* see here." Sanders got to his feet, looking leaner and meaner than he had just moments before. "You no longer have credit at this bank, or anywhere else for that matter. You already owe more on your home than the thing is worth, and you've been unemployed since late last year."

"I don't have to *work* for a living. I'm living off my investments!"

"Mr. Barnes, from what I have been able to ascertain, your investments are on life support. Now, barring a miracle, the bank is set to take your home, and I'm sorry for that, but that's just the way it is. You get yourself a job, pay down some of your other debt, and, of course, we'll be happy to talk to you again in six months' time, look into starting you off all over again."

Gruber stepped closer and placed a hand on Morton's arm. Incensed, Morton jerked his arm away from the guard.

He raised himself up to his full five-foot-nine and glared at the man. "Don't you touch me." Then he turned back to face Sanders. "When the deals I have in the works pay off and I cut all ties with this institution, it will be *you* looking for a job, Mr. Sanders, when your superiors hear of the insulting treatment you offered to one of the most prominent men in Houston. And I want you to know, when that day comes, that I aim to do all I can to see you don't find another position with another bank in the entire state of Texas."

He spun on his heel, ignored the security guard, and marched out of Sanders' office. Without looking left or right, he walked straight for the front door of the bank and out onto the sidewalk.

Late afternoon sun beat down mercilessly, making beads of sweat pop out on Morton's brow. If it wasn't for that damned wife of his lighting out, cleaning out his bank account, and scalping him in the divorce settlement, Morton wouldn't have to deal with carpetbaggers like Frederick J. Sanders.

He noticed people giving him odd looks and veering widely around him. Shaking his head, he went straight to his beloved Caddy. Ol' Bessie, here, was about the only thing that Carla hadn't demanded in the divorce, and she was for sure the only female of his acquaintance that had proven herself worth one good damn.

Morton unlocked the car and got behind the wheel. He sat for a long moment, trying to figure out what the hell he was going to do next. That day's edition of the *Houston Chronicle* lay on the seat beside him. He'd picked the thing up on his way to his appointment with Sanders. He liked to keep abreast of the business news, same as he'd always done. A good businessman kept himself in the loop every single day. One could never have too much information, as far as he was concerned.

Now, he opened the paper, deliberately bypassing the help wanted section in favor of the business section. There had been a time when the name of Morton Barnes appeared in this section of the Chronicle on a regular basis. He'd parlayed the small inheritance his father had left him into first a successful construction company and then a respectable investment brokerage business. Why, he'd had so many clients, he'd taken on three brokers just to handle the volume.

Then the economy had suffered that god-awful meltdown in September 2008, and Barnes's business had gone the way of so many others—straight into the toilet. He'd been carrying a high mortgage at the time. The value of his house dropped, the mortgage payments went up when that bastard company sold the paper on his second mortgage, and the income from his investments had tanked.

*I've spent my life doing all the right things. I'm supposed to come out on top.* That's what Morton's daddy always told him. But he'd lied. Because Morton wasn't on top. He was standing hip deep in the dog's business and on the very edge of total and complete financial ruin.

A headline caught his eye on the second page of the business section. *Dos Hombres Set To Drill Benedict Oil.*

Morton's temper flared as he scanned the article, each word an abomination to him. Those two conniving bastards Evans and Magee had netted themselves another patsy, and a big one at that. He'd been their first, of course. He'd invested good money with those two young crooks. Course, he really should have known better. At least he'd had the brains to set things to rights once things started to look bad. He'd taken bold action and recovered his own investment, with a little besides for his trouble.

Now he understood what was what. Evans and Magee had used him to get their start then made it seem as if the business was failing so he pulled out of the deal. The two of them had been tight right from the first and he, Morton, older and wiser and, by God, the better man, had ended up being the odd man out.

It wasn't fair that a couple of no-accounts from the wrong side of the tracks should prosper while he, a Barnes of the Houston Barneses, should be in desperate straits, scrambling just to try and stay afloat.

*Those two would have nothing, would be nothing were it not for me.* Blind fury gripped him. Nothing but white trash, that's all those two wildcatters were. Yet, they thrived, while he…Morton rubbed his face with both hands as the sickest dread he'd ever known filled him.

Morton folded the paper and set it on the seat beside him. He started the Caddy then eased into traffic.

All his troubles had started when he'd given that lift to those two wildcatters. It was their fault, all of it. He'd go home, pour himself a stiff one, and think. Maybe, for his luck to change, those two interlopers would have to go down.

* * * *

It seemed only good manners to invite the wildcatters in for a cup of coffee while they discussed business. Besides, she had her assayer's report in the house. Making coffee would also give her a good excuse to put some distance between herself and these two very potent testosterone makers.

"Looks like you've been busy," Ryder said.

The kitchen stood at the back of the house, and they'd walked through the main rooms to get to it.

"I have. The house needed a lot of work. Still does, come to that."

"Yeah, but it looks like the end's in sight." Colt nodded, taking his time to admire the work she'd done.

"I just have the master bedroom on the inside and the painting on the outside left to do. And getting a new well, of course."

"Likely, the original well was drilled shallow, and by the ranch hands of the day." Colt looked around the kitchen. Susan had the sense he took everything in and missed nothing. She knew that was an odd thing to think. She didn't know this man, after all. Yet something about him and his partner seemed familiar to her. Then, just that fast, she had it. They reminded her of the men in her family. *Manly men.* The kind she'd given up on finding for herself.

She forced her attention back on the conversation. "That's likely, isn't it? Turn-of-the-century ranchers tended to do it all for themselves, if they could."

"Of course," Ryder said. "If more men today did the same, the economy wouldn't be in the shape it's in. Josh said you had an assayer's report?"

"Yes. I'll just get the coffee brewing and go get it." She needed a jolt of caffeine herself. She made quick work of the preparations, and in moments, brown liquid dripped, and the scent of coffee filled the ranch kitchen. She excused herself and headed for the downstairs bedroom she'd turned into an office. She knew exactly where the report was, of course. She liked a neat and orderly office. Her entire living space always looked pristine—except for her bedroom. That she tended to keep in a state of constant chaos.

The men were both sitting at the table when she returned. They'd situated themselves so that no matter which chair she took, she'd be close to one of them.

"Alex said you could put us up in the bunkhouse. So, after we have our coffee and look at that report, just point us in the direction, and we'll get ourselves settled in," Colt said.

*Oh, dear.* "Um, actually, the bunkhouse doesn't exist anymore." Although it had the last time her brothers had come to visit. But the thing had looked rickety, and she hadn't planned on hiring any hands. She wanted a few head of cattle, and a few horses, but figured she could manage it all by herself, at least for the first while. So, she'd torn the old building down and had even stacked the lumber into two piles—what could be reused and what could be burned.

Susan figured if she did need help with anything, her brother Steven, who ran the main ranch, could send her Jed or Wayne to lend a hand, in which case they'd arrive in the morning and leave at night.

"No bunkhouse?" Ryder had said that, and he didn't look too happy about it, either.

Susan thought about the truck and rig sitting outside and realized these men likely not only really needed the work, but a place to stay as well.

"How many bedrooms you have here?" Ryder asked.

"Just three, upstairs." The words came before her brain could kick in and shut her mouth.

"Well, that's fine, then," Colt said. "Now, let's have a look at that report."

Susan handed over the papers and wondered at the ease with which this man had just invited himself and his partner into her home.

Then she mentally shrugged. It wouldn't likely take more than a couple of days at the most for them to drill her new well.

In those two days, she could seriously consider if she'd give these cowboys a test-drive or not. The way they'd flirted with her and the sly glances they'd traded made her believe they wouldn't be scandalized if she suggested they all get naked together.

Susan didn't sleep around, but she'd had a few very nice relationships. She'd developed a kind of sixth sense about whether or not men were open to the ménage experience.

Every instinct she possessed said these two would be.

Susan blinked, refocused on the present, and went perfectly still. Colt and Ryder stared at her. She recognized the lust in their eyes. Her mind said she should get up and leave them to their papers. Her body shivered and then readied itself, gleefully, to receive hot, hard cock.

"Care to tell us what you were thinking about just then, darlin'?" Colt's voice settled in the pit of her belly, sending liquid heat through her body, adding sensual fuel to her burgeoning hormonal fire.

"Not especially." Susan couldn't believe that heat bathed her cheeks and that those breathy, coy words had come from her mouth.

"You don't need to." Ryder's deep timbre affected her just as erotically as Colt's.

Susan couldn't decide what to do. The atmosphere in the room had changed. Rarely had she experienced this kind of instant, hot arousal. Her skin pebbled in anticipation, her breathing hitched, and her pussy clenched as if already trying to keep a hungry cock within its greedy grasp.

The sound of a chair scraping echoed as loud as a gunshot in the room. Susan looked up to see Colt looming over her. He looked like a man who'd made up his mind what he wanted, and what he wanted was her.

He reached out and drew her out of her chair, not stopping when she'd gained her feet, but pulling her inexorably closer to him, to his heat and his potent masculinity.

"If you want this to stop, you have to say no right now."

She would. Yes, she would, she'd only just met these men, after all, and she only had their word on it that her brothers had sent them, and…

Who was she kidding? She wasn't going to say no. Oh, God, she didn't want to say no. How long had it been since she'd felt this kind of heat and need humming through her blood?

*Never*. She'd never felt this kind of all-encompassing instant hunger for a man, and she felt it for both of them.

Colt inhaled, his eyes flared, and a very smug, very masculine smile blossomed on his lips. "Good girl. You're as hot for us as we are for you, aren't you?"

She couldn't answer, at least not in words. Only a sound emerged, a sound these two alpha males would have no trouble recognizing. The single moan of female need, of female surrender, puckered her nipples and slicked her sex. Her panties felt sodden, and she wanted them off of her body.

"That's what I thought," Colt said.

A second pair of hands fastened on her shoulders from behind. Colt's left hand was now free, and he used it to cup her face. Broad palm, long fingers, Susan shuddered with the knowledge that his one hand was enough to gather her up and gather her in.

"Yeah, you're hot. Now, let's just see how tasty you are."

## Chapter 3

Colt didn't care that they'd just met Susan Benedict. At that moment in time, he didn't even care that her brothers had more or less set them up with her. The only thing he cared about was getting her naked and between them as quickly as possible.

He moved down, moved in, and captured her lips with his. He meant to keep the kiss simple, a claiming and a tasting and a promise of things to come.

*Come.* God, the taste of her went straight to his cock. His libido soared like it hadn't done since he'd been a randy teenager bent on laying as many sweet young things as he could talk out of their panties.

She gave herself to him, opening her mouth, sucking his tongue into hers, and then giving him her own so that he knew this instant conflagration wasn't his alone.

He had to pull back, take a gulp of air, or he'd be inside her before she could draw her next breath. He sent Ryder a look the other man obviously had no trouble reading, for it took him mere seconds to tip Susan's head back and lay his mouth on hers.

Colt's fingers actually shook as he worked to lift her shirt out of his way. Her lace-covered breasts filled his hands as if they had been made for them. Her nipples hardened into tight little buds. More than anything, he wanted to suck on them, to pull them into his mouth and roll them between his tongue and the roof of his mouth and see how elongated he could make them.

Ryder raised his head and shot a one eyebrow-raised glance at Colt.

Colt nodded, and together, they quickly skimmed Susan's clothes off her. "We'll slow down, honey," he promised. "Just as soon as we've each had you."

Susan licked her lips and then proved she wanted what they wanted. "Please hurry!"

Her lips glistened red and wet, her breasts beckoned, plump with pretty pink nipples that had hardened into granite peaks. Her tiny waist flared into lusciously feminine hips. A sparkle at the side of her navel snagged his attention. He reached out and, with one finger, stroked the round little diamond-studded ornament she wore there.

"Sexy," he said, confident she knew he meant the entire package.

Susan stood between them, naked and practically vibrating, and Ryder's hands were doing a good job keeping her fires lit. Colt reached into his back pocket, yanked out his wallet, and plucked out one of the condoms he'd put there just that morning. Then he dropped his jeans and skivvies, sat on the nearest chair, and reached for Susan.

Spreading his knees, he pulled her close between them. The fingers of his left hand reached up and combed through her silky blond hair, his nails scraping her scalp gently as he brought her to his mouth. Her taste quenched a thirst too long unsatisfied, and he used his tongue to drink and drink. With his right hand, he stroked her slit and then slid a finger into her, testing her moisture.

"You're wet and tight, baby doll." Colt's words came out a little rougher than he'd intended. Something about the soft, hot woman under his hands seemed to bring out the primitive in him. He leaned forward and captured her right nipple between his lips. First his tongue and then his teeth teased that pebbled point until his fingers felt more of her juices trickling onto his fingers. He let her go with a wet plop and nuzzled the valley between her breasts. "How long has it been since you've had cock?"

She'd closed her eyes and begun to ride his fingers as they moved in and out of her. The clasp of her tunnel and the lush swelling of her pussy worked together to bring him to the very edge of ejaculation.

With his question, her eyes opened, her lips pouted. She looked down at his engorged cock. She licked her lips and reached toward it. "It's been so long. Please, I want to taste you."

"You will. But first…" His hand left her head and took up the condom. He used his teeth to tear into the foil and, with one hand, was able to roll the protection into place. He raised his gaze and noticed Ryder had dropped his clothes, rolled on his own condom.

His friend pressed himself against Susan's back then placed his hands on her waist.

"Up you go," Ryder said.

"Impale yourself on me, baby doll." Colt inhaled sharply because the scent of her juices reached him now, making him even hotter. "Give me your hot little cunt."

"First you're going to ride Colt, then I'm going to ride you." Ryder's voice, husky, strained, told Colt he was sorely triggered, too.

"You're ours, Susie Q. From this moment on. Now fuck me." The silk of her thighs slid against his, and the heat of her pussy teased, making his cock twitch in anticipation. Then he groaned in pure pleasure when the hot, tight sheath of her cunt slowly swallowed his cock.

* * * *

Susan grabbed Colt's shoulders as she lowered herself onto his cock. The thick head brushed her clit before nestling between the folds of her pussy, spreading them and surging into her with one steady thrust.

*Oh, God.* It had been so long since she'd had hot, pulsing male flesh inside her, she'd nearly forgotten the blessed fullness, the hard thrill.

*No, nothing has ever been as good as this.*

"Oh, baby, your cunt feels so damn good around my cock."

"Mmm, your cock feels pretty damn good inside me, too." Susan closed her eyes to better savor the sensations rippling through her.

Then a hot, naked male body pressed against her back. Ryder's cock nudged her, and she wanted to move against him, relish this second hard cock being offered for her pleasure.

His hands reached forward over her shoulders, grasping her breasts and squeezing them with passionate promise. Colt's hands bracketed her waist, strong and sure.

"Fuck me, Susan. Use your muscles. Squeeze me."

"Do you have any idea how hot you look, fucking him?" Ryder leaned close, and his hot, moist breath bathed her ear.

Susan imagined herself a queen with two virile sex slaves ready to service her. She loved being the center of their attention, the focus of their desire. Colt said she was theirs, but these two hard bodies were hers, and she would make the most of this wonderful opportunity. Turning herself over to them, giving them total control of her body, felt like the greatest gift she'd ever given herself.

The gentle glide and sensuous slide of hot male cock, the grip and press of hot male hands, and the sexy, hungry man-growls coming from Colt's throat all combined to send her higher and higher.

"I'm going to come, baby doll. I want to feel your hot tunnel convulse around my cock as I shoot inside you. I want to feel your cunt milk me. Come for me, baby. Come now."

Colt followed up his sexy demand by licking his thumb then running it back and forth across her clit.

Susan cried out, her climax *so* close. She wanted to come so badly. She tried to take over the rhythm of their fucking, to work herself closer to coming, but Colt controlled her completely, keeping the speed of their in and out dance languid.

Her orgasm shivered and quivered, creeping closer inch by excruciating inch.

And then Colt pinched her clit between his thumb and forefinger. "Now!"

Susan screamed as the cyclone hit, as her orgasm flooded her, roaring her heart, racing her blood, driving every thought from her head until there was only the thrill of climax, the bliss of rapture, wave after stunning wave of it.

Her arms had been gently pulled above her head, and it felt as if both men moved her, up and down, until Colt swore then clasped her even more firmly. Ryder held her down, and she felt the tip of Colt's cock tight against her cervix, the spasms and added heat as his sperm shot into the condom pushing her to the next level, pushing her to come and come and come.

He filled her and drained her, and she collapsed, the strength seeping out of her.

"Susie Q, your cunt damn near sucked me dry." Colt's words brought a smile to her face. And then she squeaked as he raised them both off the chair and carried her to the kitchen table.

He set her down, laid her flat, then stepped out from between her splayed legs. Ryder took his place. Colt left the room for a minute. It didn't take a genius IQ to figure out where he was headed.

Susan blinked, lured from the lull of satiation when Ryder grasped her legs and spread them wider. A classically vulnerable position, she couldn't deny the tiny thrill it gave her to be so exposed and, yes, so vulnerable. Colt returned from the bathroom, his gaze focused on her pussy as he made his way around the table. She now had a man at either end of her body. Two men who would do whatever they wanted to do with her. As if he'd just heard that thought, Colt reached down and drew her arms above her head, cuffing her two wrists with one hand.

Ryder ran the back of his fingers up and down across her slit.

"Mmm, is there anything more appealing than wet pussy? Let me say wet, shaved pussy. Your lips here are pink from attention." His gaze darkened, and met hers. "If you had anything planned for the rest of today and into tonight, you'll have to cancel your plans. We won't be done with you anytime soon."

She caught the expression, the sense of being dared to argue. She opened her mouth and said, "Fuck me."

Ryder shifted then thrust his cock into her, hard and fast and deep. Susan arched her back, pressing her cunt closer to him, then dipped her hips to try to rub her clit against Ryder's pubic hair. She succeeded with a soft brush, and the shiver of arousal made her gasp.

"No." Ryder used his palm to lay a stinging slap on her bare hip.

The heat of contact only served to add more fuel to her rekindled fires.

"You're not in charge here, Susie Q. Your role is to spread yourself and take what we give you, when we give it to you, in the way that we give it to you. I dare you to tell me that's not what you want."

Susan couldn't control the whimper that came out of her because that was exactly what she wanted, and thank God these men seemed to know that. So she gave him her response by spreading herself wider for him.

"Do you want me to hold her down for you?" Colt's voice had deepened. Susan turned her head, the sight of his newly re-hardened cock making her mouth water.

"Yeah. Hold her so I can ride her."

Susan's sense of humor responded to the play on his name. Before she could laugh, Colt moved.

He placed his left arm behind her knees, then pulled, bringing her legs toward her head, as if he would fold her in half. The pressure changed the angle of her slit, and Ryder's cock felt so much larger inside her.

With Colt holding her arms and legs, she couldn't move, couldn't so much as twitch her hips.

"Oh, look at that pretty little anus. You'll have our cocks there, too, soon, baby. But, right now, I'm going to fuck you…for my pleasure, not yours."

Susan cried out as her arousal surged, as Ryder began to move, his thrusts fast and furious, direct and deep. He stretched her, angling his hips so that he just missed rubbing against her clit. His plundering cock stroked her G-spot, battering her with waves of Eros she couldn't lasso, couldn't force into orgasm. Over and over, he thrust into her, and for the first time in her life, Susan experienced her secret desire—to be taken, controlled, used in a way that all she could do was take and *feel*.

"Oh, God, yes, oh, please!" Here was a kind of pleasure she'd never known, something both more and less than orgasm, something that shimmered through her in a way nothing had ever done before.

"She's so wet. I think our little Susie likes being taken hard." Ryder's gaze speared hers. His strained expression spoke of a titanic battle, and she knew he held back his own completion, savoring the same kind of pleasure she'd only just discovered.

"More." Susan closed her eyes, the pleasure becoming sharp and with such beauty that she wanted to clutch it close and hold on to it.

"You want more fucking, woman?"

Ryder's tone demanded a response. She'd thought him the shier of the two, but she'd been wrong. There was nothing shy about Ryder Magee.

"Yes, more, fuck me more, fuck me harder." How had she thought she'd known what good sex was? Susan couldn't even command her own orgasm, her body no longer belonged to her. Her body had given itself to these men completely, would only answer to their will, their whims.

"Turn your head toward Colt. I want to see what you look like with cock in your mouth."

Susan complied, her need to taste, to suck cock suddenly acute. They shifted her, a quick, short jerk that had her at the edge of the table, closer to Colt. Knowing these two wildcatters would keep her safe, she put all her attention on the cock that bobbed so close. Sensing what these men wanted, she opened her mouth.

"Yeah, that's it. Just open to us, baby, just let us have you."

Colt began to move his hips, to fuck her mouth at the same time as Ryder continued to fuck her cunt. The sounds they made met a need in her that had been buried so deep she'd never before known for certain it was there. The swirling colors of passion formed behind her closed eyes, blocking every thought until she became a vessel, *their* vessel.

"Surrender, woman. Surrender to the demands of your men. Do it, now!"

Ryder's angry sounding command washed over her. She nearly told him she'd surrendered already. In the next instant, she knew that would have been a lie. There remained one tiny part of her held back, one tiny scrap of will that longed to exercise some control, to determine the moment of purest bliss for herself. But that moment wasn't hers to steal or force. It would, it should, be a gift, from these strong men who now owned her body.

Susan cried out and tensed every muscle, relishing the sensation of cocks fucking her, using her tongue to stroke and her cunt to squeeze. And then she let it all go, relaxed, gave over.

"Yeah, that's right. You're ours!"

Susan's body erupted into an orgasm more intense, more exciting than anything she could have imagined. Colt's cock began to pulse in her mouth, and she drank gulp after gulp of his ejaculation as she felt Ryder's cock quiver inside her pussy. And when he held himself deep, when he poured himself into her, she clenched her inner muscles, drawing the hot male essence if not into her body, then into her very soul.

# Chapter 4

The men had no trouble locating her bedroom, which was a good thing, Susan mused. She might have managed a grunt and a point, but that would have been it. She tried not to give too much credence to the shiver of pleasure that raced down her spine when Ryder scooped her into his arms and simply carried her up the stairs as if she had been a petite miss.

He didn't ask, just carried her into the shower. Like most of the bathrooms in most of the Benedict homes, this one hosted a shower and a spa that would each hold four to six adults, easily.

When she'd ordered the fixtures, it hadn't occurred to her to have it any other way, even though she'd thought she'd given up on finding men of her own.

Ryder adjusted his hold on her, and she immediately put her arms around his neck while her legs dangled. She heard him working the faucet then felt the warmth of water raining down on her.

"Some shower you've got here, Ms. Benedict."

Susan smiled. "Glad you like it."

The glass door slid open. "Well, now, room for us to play."

Colt shut the door, and the heat and steam began to build. Ryder lowered her and turned her around. *Ohh, I'm about to become the filling in a man sandwich.* Her gaze slid to the high shelf when Colt grabbed the bar of soap. She spied several small foil packets that hadn't been there last night when she'd showered.

"Let's see how you feel under our wet and soapy hands." Colt handed the bar of soap to Ryder and then set to washing her. His hands boldly caressed her breasts, cupping and squeezing as if they belonged to him. It felt so good, she nearly melted. But she wanted to be an active participant in water sports.

"I want to touch, too." It pleased her to put just a tiny pout in her tone. She felt lax and loose and tired, but curiously energized, too.

"I don't believe anyone is stopping you, sweetheart." Ryder's deep rumble rattled around in her belly, tickling her clit and making her juices flow.

He held the soap over her shoulder then let it drop. Susan caught it and wasted no time lathering her hands then setting the soap back on its shelf. Shivers wracked her as Ryder began massaging her back, and she wondered for a moment if she'd be able to do what she wanted, right at that moment, to do.

Grabbing hold of her self-discipline, she reached out with both hands, one in front and one behind, and wrapped her fingers around hot, turgid male cocks.

The men's hands faltered, and Susan felt her smile slide just this side of sultry as she slid her closed fists up and then down, the water and the slippery soap aiding her in giving the men a taste of their own teasing.

"God in heaven, Ms. Benedict, you have a fine touch," Colt said as sucked in a breath.

"Like I'm being stroked by an angel," Ryder said.

"She has the mouth of an angel, too," Colt said.

This wasn't Susan's first ménage, but it certainly was the first with men who seemed so suited to it and so perfectly at ease with it.

"Gentlemen, your choreography leads me to believe I'm not the first woman you've shared."

"It's not nice to kiss and tell," Colt said. He lifted the shower wand and rinsed her breasts. "Let's just say we never take on a project without having a pretty good idea what's involved, first."

"I'm a project?" Susan gave them just enough extra pressure to ensure they knew she was just a little ticked with that comparison.

"The sweetest kind."

"I see."

Colt reached for the soap, lathered his hands again. She could see he flicked a glance at Ryder and wondered what they were thinking. Before she could ask, every thought dissolved as he cupped her pussy and began to rub.

He lifted her hand from his cock. Ryder extricated himself easily, too, and she knew it wasn't just her thoughts that had deserted her. She'd enjoyed sex in the past, on occasion. She'd never gone weak-kneed before.

"You know, honey, you play your cards right, we might see our way clear to giving you a discount."

Ryder's words shocked her, a fine line of outrage that grew and swirled to gigantic proportions in mere seconds.

"Why, you son of a..."

Colt laughed and spun her around. Ryder combed his fingers into the short, wet strands of her hair and yanked her close. His mouth took hers in a kiss that was instantly hot, totally carnal. Susan sank into the kiss, drinking him, reveling in him.

In total control, Ryder broke the kiss but left his hands in her hair. Downward pressure told her what he wanted before his words did.

"On your knees, woman. Suck me off."

She'd tasted Colt and discovered a new addiction. Slowly, she slithered down and prepared to discover another.

* * * *

"Yeah, just like that." Ryder closed his eyes as Susan Benedict showed him a glimpse of heaven. Her mouth, hot and wet, surrounded his cock. Her tongue stroked up and down his shaft with slow, lusty strokes. He spread his fingers in her hair and couldn't resist the urge to pump into her mouth just a little.

She immediately surrendered control, loosening her suction just enough that he could freely, and oh so sexily, fuck her mouth at whatever pace he chose.

"You do look good with cock in your mouth, Susie Q," Colt said.

Her hum of pleasure at his friend's compliment felt fucking fantastic on his dick.

Colt finished his shower and left them, but Ryder didn't worry he'd been miffed. Ryder put his attention back on the gorgeous woman kneeling before him.

"You have a great mouth, honey. Will you drink me?" He'd have thought he couldn't come again so soon, but this woman turned him on more than any he'd been with in a long, long time. He could feel his seed collecting as his balls got heavier, and he knew it wouldn't take much of Susan Benedict's particular brand of lip service before he erupted.

She answered him with a soft hum of assent and the gentle cupping of his scrotum in her right hand.

Ryder shouted out as, hot, fast, volcanic, the climax exploded out of him, stream after stream that seemed to draw strength and vitality from every part of him. He couldn't help the way his fingers gripped her head, the way he held her there so she would be forced to swallow even as he understood she did so willingly, even eagerly.

He shook from the force of the pleasure she'd given him, weakened in a way he rarely had been. Spent, he locked his knees, willing back his strength, needing to remain standing, and more, needing to be able to lift this angel into his arms.

Even though he'd finished, she continued to suck him, tapering her draw, until she slid his now flaccid dick from between her lips.

She looked at his cock for a long moment, then bent forward and placed a kiss on the tip. Ryder swallowed hard as his heart turned over in his chest.

It came to him slowly that the water had turned cool. He reached forward, turned it off. Then he reached down and lifted Susan up and into his arms.

"You're very strong to be able to do that," she said.

"You don't weigh much." He waited until her gaze met his. "Thank you." The kiss he gave her felt reverent to him, because it was.

"You're welcome." Her smile reminded him of peaches, her cheeks bloomed just that much.

Carefully, he stepped from the shower stall with her in his arms. Colt waited for them, a fluffy towel in his hands. He had no problem turning her over to his best friend. Colt kissed her then set her on her feet.

Ryder snagged another towel and helped Colt dry Susan, then ran it quickly over his own body. Colt scooped her up again and carried her across the hall to her bedroom. Ryder stood back and watched as Colt laid their woman on her bed.

"I've been snooping," his friend admitted.

"Have you now?" She raised herself on her elbows and shook her head, tossing her still damp hair behind her and off her face. Her pretty brown eyes sparkled as if she'd just spied the presents under the Christmas tree. Raising her left eyebrow, and in a tone that mocked snobbery, she asked, "And what did you find in your snooping?"

"A veritable bounty of goodies," his friend replied. He slid open the drawer in the bedside table, then met Ryder's gaze. "Would you like the handcuffs or the lube?"

Ryder had rarely seen such a Cheshire-cat grin on a woman's face. "Well, now," Ryder said, "I think I'll let you have first choice." He took a moment to slide his gaze over to Susan. She lay there on the bed pretty much how Colt had left her, spread out, a feast awaiting their consumption. "I'm still feeling pretty damn satisfied, myself."

Colt nodded then reached into the drawer and pulled out a black and white tube, the brand name a rainbow of colors. He skewered Susan with a stare.

"Is this unopened because you ran out or because you've never had a cock in your ass?"

Ryder's gaze was fastened on the intriguing woman, and so he caught the flare of heat in her expression and the fine tremor that shook her.

He looked down. The sight of her cunt glistening restored his cock, making it harden faster than any time he could ever recall.

"It's a new tube."

"Baby," Colt began to unscrew the top of the tube, "you like having your ass played with? Having a cock buried deep in your anus? Having two cocks inside you at the same time, one in your ass and one in your cunt?"

Susan shuttered her eyes for just a moment. Her cheeks glowed anew. Ryder thought he was beginning to understand her. The lady obviously didn't play fast and loose, but she did play, and enjoyed it.

"No," she said at last. "I don't like any of that stuff. I *love* it."

Ryder caught the tone. He looked at Colt, then back at Susan.

"You love it, and you've been waiting for just the right two men…men who won't damage you, but won't coddle you, either. Would that be an accurate assessment?"

The look of longing on her face made him want to throttle every man who'd ever thought himself good enough to have her. How could they have been with her and not understood, instantly, what she needed, what she so obviously craved?

"Yes. *Yes*. I'm not some delicate flower to be treated as if I'd break at any moment." Had she meant to reveal to them just how desperate she was for proper loving? Probably not, Ryder thought. But she had, and as far as Ryder was concerned, that was just fine. He planned to give her everything she needed and wanted and then some.

"Toss me the handcuffs." He heard the edge in his own voice. Had he just thought he'd been satisfied? His cock reared up, hot and strong, as if sensing cunt for the first time in years.

He caught the shiny steel then took one step forward. "Do you have a paddle?"

Susan's nipples hardened at that question. She licked her lips. "No."

"You will have." Two steps took him to the bed. He put one knee on the bed then reached down, took her hands, brought her wrists together, stretching them out over her head. The brass bedstead looked solid. He cuffed her in a way that would allow for her to turn onto her side…or get up onto her knees, however he and Colt decided to move her and take her.

Colt set the tube down then reached back into the drawer. He tossed a box of condoms onto the table. It, too, was brand new. His friend had the twelve-pack open in seconds. "This will let us get started. We have more in the truck."

"We're going to take you the way you've needed to be taken." Ryder shot Colt a look, then leaned down and kissed Susan's left nipple.

"But first, we're going to make you come so much and scream so hard that all you'll be able to do afterward is just lie there and let us take you, over and over again." He thought she looked as if she'd come right there on the spot from his words alone. Ryder had just about given up ever finding a woman who'd let him and his best friend unleash their inner beasts. And here she was, lying open and ready before them.

"You're ours now, Susan Benedict." Colt's voice shook with excitement. "And we're about to show you just exactly what that means."

Susan's response was to spread her legs and bend her knees. "Yes, I'm yours."

Ryder thought those were the sexiest three words he'd heard in his entire life.

* * * *

Nothing disappointed Susan more than apologetic lovers. It had taken only moments with Colt and Ryder to understand these men were different from every man she'd ever taken into her body.

Not that there had been a lot of them, of course. In her life, she'd experienced one long-term relationship with a single male in college, and then a couple of not-quite-as-long-term ménages. In each case, she'd been left wanting, needing more than they were willing, or able, to give her.

The way Colt kept his gaze on hers while he pressed a generous amount of lube onto his fingers…thank God, *finally*, men who would take what she so desperately wanted to give and give what she needed more than her next breath.

He tossed aside the tube, leaned forward, gave her anus a couple of strokes. And then, *yes*, he pushed one long, thick finger hard against that opening, spearing her, entering her, all the way in.

"Ahh!" Susan came in an explosion of bliss, her anus clenching over and over as it sought more of the fabulous friction Colt gave her when he began to finger-fuck her ass.

Ryder knelt beside her and stroked her clit, making that tiny nub go hard. She pushed her hips up, needing more. Ryder grunted, then covered her cunt with his mouth.

Lips, tongue, teeth, they all tasted her, nibbled her. She dripped from his oral attentions, and she knew it wasn't all from him, that moisture. Colt finger-fucked her ass in a strong, steady rhythm while Ryder ate her pussy. Susan tugged on the handcuffs and came again. Every muscle in her body tensed, and she drew down and drew tight, holding the delicious sensations of orgasm, the quiver and the shiver and the gush.

"You taste good, woman. You're such a hot little piece. Let's see how much more you can take."

She opened her eyes and watched Colt get more lube, coating two fingers. He gave her the devil's grin when he extended those fingers toward her. Without hesitation, he inserted both fingers into her ass. Ryder put two fingers together, said, "Her pussy's so sopping wet, we don't need lube here," and inserted them into her cunt.

Both men worked their fingers in and out of her, the motion fast and furious. Ryder bent down, used his tongue to find her clit, and sucked it into his mouth.

"Oh, God!" Susan came, the sensation so electric that she thought her pussy might just go numb with it.

"You love that." Ryder's voice always seemed to affect her low in her belly.

"Yes!" Eyes closed, it was all she could say. Words seemed so far away from what she felt capable of at the moment.

Then she heard the unmistakable sound of plastic tearing.

"On your knees, Susan. I'm going to fuck that pretty ass of yours now."

Colt's command shivered down her back, but the men gave her no time to respond. They turned her over then lifted her so that she had no choice but to get her knees under her.

"You're so fucking ready for me." He moved over her, and she felt the heat of his body tenting her. The brush of his latex-covered cock against her anus made her moan, the head feeling hot and hard despite the protective cover as it nudged her opening.

"Yeah, that's it. You want to feel my cock sink into your ass, don't you, Susie?" He gripped her ass cheeks in his big, powerful hands and spread them.

"Beg me, baby. Beg me to fuck your ass."

No man had dared treat her this way, yet this was exactly how she'd always dreamed of being treated. Not like a delicate flower, but like a woman, a woman to be used to give pleasure as well as to be pleasured.

"Please. Oh, please, fuck me. Fuck my ass…*yes*!"

She felt his cock press against her and then sink deep. Colt grunted, the sound calling to her feminine animal, a sound of pleasure and greed.

"I'm going to ride you baby. Nice and hard."

She had nothing to grasp, could do nothing but let go of the muscles in her hips and legs and take the reaming he gave her. In and out in a steady pace, not delicate, not tentative, but strong, sure, with throaty hums and guttural groans to let her know how good she felt to him. The sensation of his engorged cock moving in and out of her pushed her arousal impossibly high. Nothing had ever felt so good. She needed more, the rough possession stirring her arousal in a way she'd never imagined, a way that seemed to be everywhere at once, a way that turned every inch of her body, every angle, every plane, every surface into one big erogenous zone.

"You look so good with cock in your ass." Ryder bent down. "I'm getting so hard watching him fuck your ass, Susie Q. I can hardly wait until it's my turn, until we're both inside you, fucking you, coming in you."

"You were made to have our cocks in your ass, baby," Colt grunted in cadence with his thrusts. "Yeah, that's it, let go and just surrender. Loosen those muscles and just take it. Mmm, yes, take it all."

The slap of his balls against her slit made her pussy sizzle. Colt increased his rhythm, his cock moving in and out of her so fast, she felt her clit and her G-spot both tingling, that place deep down where his cock hit bottom tingling, until she knew she was going to come, and come hard.

She couldn't contain it, could do nothing but lay there, her face to the side, her shoulders pushed onto the bed, the entire bed shaking with the force of his thrusts.

"Oh, God, yes, yes, what a sweet ass, woman. *Yes!*"

The sensations of Colt's cock pulsing in her ass pushed her over the edge. Susan screamed as she came, screamed as the storm of her orgasm caught her and held her, as wave after wave of pure, undiluted rapture burned her from the inside out. She screamed and screamed until she wondered if the bliss wouldn't make her pass out.

## Chapter 5

Susan awoke lying on her stomach. The sensation of hands moving down her back, caressing her ass, then stroking up again felt good. "Mmm," she said.

"She lives," Ryder said.

Susan laughed. "Oh, yeah. I'm alive."

"I didn't hurt you, sweetheart?" Colt asked.

"No. It just felt so good." Susan shivered recalling just how good it had felt to have his cock in her ass.

"So, you're not too sore?"

Susan turned her head at the hopefulness she heard in Ryder's voice. "Too sore for what?" She tried to contain her smile, but couldn't. Oh, she knew what he wanted. It was the same thing she wanted.

"Too sore for some more anal play."

"Never." Yes, she felt tender. It had been a long time since she'd enjoyed anal sex, and even then, in the past, it had been…well, it had been so *wimpy*. Colt hadn't been wimpy, he'd been masterful. Oh, God, it had been wonderful, and tender or not, she wanted to experience that again.

"On your side, sweetheart. I want you to face Colt. In fact," Ryder moved her onto her side the way he'd just ordered and then ran his tongue along the shell of her ear, "I want your arms around him, and I want you to kiss him."

Colt slipped his arm around her waist and eased her left leg over his hips. She put her arms around his neck and stretched up for his kiss.

His flavor sank into her, a ripe flavor that reminded her of racing on horseback across the open range, wind in her hair, all tethers gone. He tasted wild and sinful, and she knew she'd be able to recognize him simply by his taste.

Ryder leaned over her, his fingers spreading a bit more lube up and down over her anus and then pushing into her.

"Mm, you opened for me just like a beautiful flower." His words brushed her neck, a dark pleasure that shivered through her even as Colt's tongue continued to stroke and play with her own and Ryder's fingers moved in and out of her.

Colt pinched one nipple, and she moaned, her hips flexing forward and then back to take Ryder's fingers even deeper.

"You're so ready for me," Ryder said.

She felt him loom over her from behind. Then his fingers slipped out, and his latex-covered cock pressed against her opening, pressed and then slid into her, solid and deep.

"My God, woman, you have an incredible ass, so hot and tight and good. You're so perfect for us." Ryder began a slow, steady glide and slide in and out of her.

Susan moaned. Her lips left Colt's because she needed to stretch and move, she needed to draw in air and savor the eroticism of this, the uncontrolled passion of her body as it climbed the ladder of Eros.

"You are perfect for us," Colt said. "Your pussy needs my fingers, doesn't it, baby?" He gave her no time to answer. He simply began to move them in and out of her cunt.

"Oh, God, *yes*." The sensations growing in her were completely outside of her control. She couldn't force them or hold them back. They had taken on life of their own, fueled by the incredible sensation of Ryder's cock moving in and out of her ass in a sure and steady rhythm and Colt's fingers plundering her pussy at the same speed.

She closed her eyes and totally surrendered herself to their possession.

"God, what a beautiful look on your face." Ryder's tone sounded strained, and his breath quivered as he inhaled. "I'm close, baby. I wanted to savor this longer. Your ass feels so damn good. But I need to come."

"Very soon, you're going to have us in you at the same time," Colt said. "I think you're nearly stretched enough for us both. Do you want that? Do you want to have our cocks fucking you at the same time?"

*More than anything.* She couldn't speak the words, though, she could only whimper, because arousal became electric currents, little shock waves that sprouted and zapped, that teased and called to her, that moved with no pattern over her entire body, electrifying her very soul.

"Oh, God." She could gasp those words, and hoped they understood.

"You do want that." Ryder leaned over, closer, so that his words and his breathing, quicker now, bathed the side of her face.

"Mmm." Susan's eyes opened, widening as the spiraling sensations within her grew and grew. So close, her orgasm gathered, but then ebbed. A fine lunacy, she thought, and those words seemed perfect to describe her state. She could only lie there and let these incredibly manly men do whatever they wanted to her.

"I'm going to pound in you, baby. I have to. I need…" Ryder's voice dropped off, his head rested on her shoulder, and he began to thrust harder and faster in her. Yes, she needed that, too. She felt primitive, changed, now a purely physical being. She moved, jutting her ass toward Ryder, resting her head on Colt's chest.

Colt held her fast, held her still, so that all she could do was take what Ryder gave her. Fast and furious now, he moved, his grunts and cries signaling his desperate race to completion.

Colt's fingers eased from her cunt, then grasped her clit and pinched hard.

"*Oh, God!*" Cataclysmic climax exploded inside her, shattering her into a million tiny shards of quivering bliss, a volcanic eruption of ecstasy more violent than anything she'd ever experienced. Every atom of her body shivering in the purest rapture she'd ever known.

She felt Ryder's cock, buried deep in her ass, pulsing his orgasm, and heard in his grunts and groans that his pleasure matched hers, a pleasure so acute it bordered on torture.

Her climax ebbed, and she shivered, a teeth rattling, bone jarring shiver she hadn't expected and couldn't stop.

"Colt."

"I've got her."

She heard their voices, but they seemed impossibly far away. She closed her eyes, aware, but far too zoned, to react. The bed dipped behind her, and if she could, she would have smiled at the stumbling gait of her lover as he headed for the bathroom. Colt's arms surrounded her, the furnace-like heat of his body slowly thawing her numbness. It seemed only seconds later the bed dipped again. Another furnace heated her from behind. Naked male flesh in front and back of her soothed her shattered senses.

"Thank you, Angel." Ryder's words and the kiss he placed on her shoulder warmed her heart.

"Sleep now, baby," Colt said.

Susan felt herself falling and, feeling safe between them, let herself go.

\* \* \* \*

Colt rolled to his right side and propped his head up on his hand. Beside him, Susan Benedict slept soundly on her stomach, her face turned toward him, the sound of her breathing a soft puff of air that teased his skin. The sheet just barely covered her ass, leaving the sleek shape of her—the plump pillows of her breasts and the sweet dip of her hips—temptingly reachable. Next to her, taking up the last third of the very large bed, Ryder, head burrowed under his pillow, snored softly. Narrowing his eyes, Colt focused on the clock on the night table beside his best friend. The green LED display read two-fifteen.

Colt's belly rumbled, reminding him that he and his best friend had been so busy having the delectable Susan, they hadn't any of them stopped to have dinner. Considering the liberties he'd taken with Ms. Benedict's body, he didn't think she'd mind if he helped himself to the contents of her fridge.

With subtle movements, he eased himself from the bed. He stood back and watched his woman sleep. There existed no doubt within him at all. Susan Benedict belonged to him—to him and Ryder. At least, she did for now. His narrow-eyed gaze took in the entirety of the bed. In his sleep, Ryder moved closer to Susan, his arm slipped over her hip. Even so, Colt figured there was enough room in that bed for at least two more people.

He'd heard whispers about the Benedicts since before he'd met them. He'd also heard tales about their hometown of Lusty, Texas. Judging by both the bed and the shower, it would seem those whispers had merit. He wondered if on some level that wasn't why he and Ryder had hit it off so well with Josh and Alex the first time they had met.

It certainly explained that unusual meeting they'd had with the brothers a couple of days ago.

He snagged his boxers from among the scattered clothes on the floor and quickly pulled them on. He didn't bother with shoes or socks, a decision he regretted just a few moments later when he padded outside to the truck.

Neither he nor Ryder had packed much for this particular job. They'd figured the drilling would likely take a couple of days, and the other not-so-subtle request that they see what they could do to coax Ms. Benedict out of her emotional slump in whatever way they could, just a few more. So they'd each stashed a duffel bag in the small storage space in the back of the cab, enough clothes for maybe a week—and a box of condoms, just in case.

Colt grabbed both bags, then locked the truck.

Inside the house, he set their bags by the stairs and headed into the kitchen to see what he could find to eat. He hoped the lady wasn't a vegetarian because he had a yen for some meat. A sandwich would do, for now.

He found everything he could have hoped for, including what appeared to be homemade bread.

If the lady sleeping so sexily upstairs made her own bread, he didn't see how he and Ryder would ever be able to let her go.

*Whoa.* Colt never thought the words "permanent" and "woman" in the same sentence. *Best put a lid on that kind of thinking.*

"My gut woke me up, too."

Colt jerked his gaze to the doorway as Ryder, also sporting only his boxers, came into the kitchen.

"There's roast beef and homemade bread."

"I need coffee." Ryder investigated the caffeine possibilities and quickly put a pot on to brew.

"The smell of that's going to wake her," Colt commented as the scent of coffee filled the air.

"That wouldn't be a hardship," Ryder said.

Colt chuckled. "No, but we could at least pretend to be gentlemen and let the lady get a full night's sleep."

"Gentlemen are so overrated," Susan said.

She looked sexy as hell wearing nothing but a T-shirt that came down to mid-thigh. Her blond hair, rumpled and pillow dried, just added to her appeal.

She moved to the cupboard and brought down three cups.

"I don't know," Colt said, shaking his head as she reached for the coffeepot. "The last time we sat down here to have coffee, all heaven broke loose."

"Smooth talker." Susan poured the brew and passed the cups around. "I'd intended to pull one of my mother's frozen lasagnas out of the freezer and bake it for our dinner."

"Colt and I are both pretty good cooks."

Ryder's comment told him more than just the sum total of the words. Neither of them had ever offered to cook for a woman before. Cooking implied a deeper level of relationship than either of them had been willing to offer so far.

Blood will tell, and neither one of them had what you could call respectable parentage. They'd never felt they could offer a woman more than a few days of fun.

Colt couldn't say why he'd sensed right from the first moment that Susan Benedict was going to be different. He just had, and now, he knew Ryder felt the same.

"Well, good. You know, I woke up, and the two of you were gone, but I knew you hadn't gone far. And then I started thinking."

"You don't appear to me to be the sort of woman who ever stops. Thinking, that is." Colt shot a quick look at Ryder, wondering if his friend was getting any "pissed off" vibes from the lady. He himself wasn't, but he'd never claimed to be particularly intuitive when it came to women and their emotions.

"Thank you." Susan smiled at them both then tilted her head to one side. "Just how well do you know my brothers?"

Ryder lifted both his eyebrows as he sent Colt a pointed look. Colt shrugged.

"We've known Josh and Alex socially for a few years. Recently, we've become business partners."

Susan raised one eyebrow. "How recently?"

Colt hesitated only for a heartbeat. "Very."

"Huh."

Susan pulled out a chair and positioned herself between them. She sipped her coffee slowly, and Colt didn't really know what would happen next. Her brothers had suggested that since he and Ryder were single and their sister also single, and since they, her brothers, recognized Susan as a mature, fully grown adult woman capable of deciding on her own friends…Come to think of it, neither Alex nor Josh had actually finished that thought.

It's not as if they'd been awarded the contract with Benedict Oil and Minerals as a payoff for services of a more personal nature about to be rendered.

*Then why the hell does it feel that way?*

"What does that mean, exactly? That 'huh'?" Colt asked.

She gave him her undivided attention. Then she gave him a smile that was slow, sultry, and maybe a little smug.

"Men get so nervous when women make non-distinct vocal sounds," Susan said.

"That's only because the first caveman discovered that a grunt from his woman meant, 'you have to sleep sometime, sucker'," Colt said. "As a species, we've been on our guard ever since."

Susan burst into peals of laughter that settled inside Colt in a way he'd never experienced before.

She turned her pretty brown gaze toward Ryder. "Would you care to add a comment at this time?"

"Hell, no. What he said." Ryder pointed to Colt. "Beyond that, I'm keeping my mouth shut."

"Thanks a lot, partner."

"Anytime, partner."

Susan shook her head, then put her cup down. "Well, in this case, 'huh' means that, apparently, my brothers had a hand in bringing us together, and not only so that I could get my well drilled. I'm trying to decide how I feel about that."

Colt shifted in his chair, the feeling of having been dishonest—if only by omission—playing hell with his conscience.

"Damn," Ryder muttered.

"Yeah." Colt nodded to him. Then he gave Susan what he hoped was his best smile. "I guess we'd better come clean."

Her smile ebbed, and she sat back in her chair. Colt had the sense that she braced herself for bad news.

"Yes," she said at last. "I guess you'd better."

## Chapter 6

"So they didn't exactly set you up," Colt said. "The way I see it, the only real thing they did was send us here. What happened once we arrived, the three of us did on our own."

Susan wasn't surprised that Alex and Josh had sent these two wildcatters her way. She *had* asked them to recommend someone who could drill a new well for her. Yet there was something else, some wisp of a thought floating around in her mind. She didn't know why the memory was proving so elusive. She usually had no trouble recalling things and wished she could grab hold of whatever seemed to be rattling her chain.

It was there, and then it wasn't. In the meantime, Colt's conclusion pretty much matched with her own feelings.

"I agree," she said. She picked up the sandwich Ryder had put together for her and took a bite, chewing slowly. "The question is, what happens next?"

"This is more than just sex," Ryder said, the words swift and sure. "I've had sex before. This is different. I just don't know what it means."

"We're feeling possessive when that isn't something that usually enters into the equation for us," Colt said. "This isn't our first ménage experience. We both get turned on having a woman between us. We always have. I feel the same way Ryder does—this isn't just sex. Nothing ever felt like what we shared earlier."

Susan liked to believe she could tell when someone was handing her a line. The fact that both of these very macho Texan men could say what they did, squirming the entire time, told her they were being as honest with her as they knew how to be.

"How much do you know about my family?" She thought it a valid question. Where another woman might have difficulty coming to terms with having two men inside her body at the same time, Susan didn't.

"You mean other than the obvious," Colt said. "Honestly? Not much. We've heard things, but neither of us really pays much attention to gossip."

Susan ate some more of her sandwich as she tried to understand the emotions coursing through her. How ironic that just when she'd taken herself off to this corner of Texas to learn how to live on her own, just when she'd come to the conclusion there were no manly men left, that she would meet two men who could likely talk her into anything.

Susan knew what she wanted to happen next. "I want more." Had she meant to blurt it out quite so boldly? Probably. She shook her head. "Even though I realize now that you're more than just simple wildcatters, that you don't likely *need* the work here. I was going to offer you day work after the well was drilled just to keep you around. I want more."

"That's a coincidence," Colt said. His voice had gone low and soft. "We'd planned for a week, not seriously believing we'd want more."

"But we do want more," Ryder said. "I want to explore whatever this is, this pull between us." Ryder looked from her to his partner.

"So do I," Colt said. "And the fact that I do scares the hell out of me. I'm not looking for forever." He sat forward, laid his hands flat on the table.

Susan looked at those hands. They were a man's hands and, in that, similar to Ryder's. Hands that were like her fathers'. She focused on those hands. Broad and long, the palms work-roughened and capable. Though he'd mentioned being frustrated being kept behind a desk or in the boardroom, there remained enough calluses on those palms to attest to the fact he wasn't a lazy man.

Neither of them could ever be considered lazy or soft. She bet if she offered them money to stay, to help her work around the place, they'd throw it back in her face.

"I'm not looking for forever," Colt repeated. "But this is more than a one-night stand. And by the way, we don't need the money, so don't even *think* you're going to pay us for lending you a hand around here—and that includes drilling your new well."

Susan read implacability in Colt and saw the same fierce emotion reflected in Ryder's expression. They both seemed pretty adamant that they weren't interested in a lifetime commitment. Truthfully, it was a little soon to be looking for one in any event.

She narrowed her eyes and said, "If I don't pay you for drilling the well with cash, it's going to feel as if I'm paying for it another way."

"You're smarter than that, Susie Q," Ryder said. Then he grinned.

"We've been looking for an excuse to get our hands dirty again," Colt said. "We're wildcatters down to the bone."

"I've seen your bones," Susan quipped. "And I'm still going to pay you for the well."

"Fine." Colt's acceptance lacked grace. "Then we're going to grab some groceries tomorrow. You're not going to pay us and feed us, too."

"Fine." Susan understood men well enough to know these two were going to be a handful—and they likely packed hefty appetites. Thinking of appetites, images of the way she'd spent the afternoon and most of the night flashed through her mind. The dull ache between her legs turned from one of overexertion to one of longing. She tried to stifle her smile but knew she failed when both men looked at her with lust in their eyes.

Not one to totally deny the natural coquette within her, she slowly stood, then stretched. Oh, yeah. Neither man could take his eyes off her, their gazes tracking between her very hardened nipples and the bit of pussy she knew peeked out from the hem of her shirt.

"I think we should go back to bed. It's late."

Colt and Ryder exchanged a look she couldn't read. Then Colt stepped forward and blithely scooped her into his arms. The move surprised a squeak out of her. Susan threw her arms around his neck to hold on, even though she did trust him enough not to drop her.

"Bed sounds good," Colt said. "Overrated or not, we are going to be gentlemen and let you get some sleep. At least for a few hours." He mounted the stairs one at a time as if she weighed nothing at all.

"And if I don't want to sleep?"

"You will," both Colt and Ryder said at the same time.

Susan felt her right eyebrow go up and wondered that neither man seemed to notice it. Manly men. Yep, they were going to be a handful.

* * * *

Morning was just a whole lot of interesting. Having fallen asleep despite her best intentions of waiting a few minutes and seducing her lovers into an encore performance, she awoke to an empty bed and the smell of coffee once more permeating the air.

"Well, hell." Susan sat up, the sheet pooling at her waist. She ran a hand through her hair as she sat in the middle of her very rumpled bed. Just there, under the coffee, the scent of sex teased her senses. Immediately, she felt her nipples harden and her slit slicken.

She'd always enjoyed sex. Now, she felt as if, in a single evening—all right, afternoon and evening—those two wildcatters had gone and addicted her not only to the activity but to them. The least they could have done was to be on hand to give her some wake-up nookie.

Sighing heavily, she swept the sheet off herself completely and headed to the bathroom. If she wasn't going to start her morning with a satisfying session of mattress aerobics, she might as well have a hot shower and begin her day clean.

Eyes closed, she basked in the luxury of hot steaming water pelting her from four separate nozzles. The heat so relaxed her she didn't immediately notice the sound of the slide of glass.

Large male hands slid around her from behind, cupping her breasts and squeezing them. Long, talented fingers plucked her nipples, pulling them, making them stretch impossibly long.

"Colt." She could already tell the difference between the feel of their hands.

"I'm impressed, sweetheart. And touched."

She smiled and listened to her inner imp. "Well, I had a fifty-fifty chance of guessing right."

"Minx." He slapped her ass lightly. The tiny sting sent a zing of arousal straight to her pussy.

It looked like she was going to get that wake-up nookie after all. Susan sighed and relaxed in Colt's arms, laying her head back against his shoulder.

"Ryder started cooking breakfast as soon as we heard the shower come on. So we've got about a half hour before it's ready. Any idea how we could pass that time?"

"Maybe we could play poker." Susan couldn't keep the smile out of her voice.

"An excellent idea, if we had all-plastic cards." Colt began to smooth his hands over her body, caressing her breasts, rubbing low over her belly.

It took her a moment to realize he'd palmed her rose-scented soap. The subtle aroma of the lather teased her as effectively as his hands did.

"Any other ideas?" Colt's hands continued to wreak havoc with her senses.

When he slipped the soap between her legs and used it to tease and caress her slit, Susan felt her knees give way, and she groaned.

"Well?" Colt's whispered words stroked the shell of her ear, always a huge turn-on for her.

"Um, now that you mention it, something else *is* coming to mind."

"Honey, I'm sorry to tell you this, but that's not where it's going to come."

Susan laughed, Colt's dry rejoinder tickling her sense of humor like nothing else had in a long time.

In the next moment, she groaned, for he'd taken advantage of her distraction and slipped two fingers inside her pussy.

"Let me know if the soap stings." He continued to move his fingers in and out in a slow, deliberate rhythm.

"No it's…mmm." Her thoughts scattered as he finger-fucked her cunt. Arousal became a slow climb, smoke gently unfurling from the source, rising to the ceiling.

"Open more." He moved back, giving her room. She didn't even pause to consider. Her body complied with his demand instantly.

"Now, bend over just a bit…my, yes, what a delectable ass you have, Ms. Benedict."

Susan wondered if he was going to fuck her ass. She turned her head and looked at him over her shoulder. Colt's expression reflected absolute focus as his gaze stayed glued on her wet, naked flesh.

"Do you want to fuck my ass, lover?"

"Mm, yes. And I will. But right now I want your cunt. I want to take you from behind as you bend over for me."

She watched as he grabbed a condom, tore it open with his teeth. Something about that action alone, the almost feral edge to it, gave her arousal a boost.

As he rolled the protection into place, Susan couldn't help but shift her gaze to his rigid and eager-looking cock. She smiled as she recalled the oft-repeated cliché that size didn't matter.

Personally, she thought that saying must have originally been coined by someone with a small dick. She loved being stretched, loved the feeling of fullness she'd only ever experienced with one lover before these two wildcatters strutted into her life.

Colt didn't waste any time. The instant he had the condom in place, he used his left hand to position himself, grabbed her hips, and plunged.

"Oh!" With her pussy so slick, he slid easily into her, and yet the sensation of being stretched, of being so completely filled, surprised her. The memories of the day before somehow hadn't prepared her for the richness of being really well fucked. *It's the angle*. That was the only clear thought she had, and then her mind stopped wasting its precious resources on anything as mundane as thinking and focused on relishing the sensations instead.

Susan closed her eyes, stretched one hand out to brace herself against the wall, then began to clench and release her pelvic floor muscles. The friction of his cock pistoning in and out of her, hard and fast, heated her blood and stoked the pyre of her passion. His fingertips dug into her hips, making his grip even more solid as he increased his tempo. She was so very close, she could feel the shivers, the tiny electric-like tingles that always signaled impending climax.

Daring and determined, she moved her left hand to her cunt, to the place they were joined. With practiced ease, she sought her clit and began to rub it back and forth.

"Oh, God!" The explosion of her orgasm felt huge as it erupted, spreading hot flames throughout her entire body. Her tunnel felt as if it clenched in spasmodic chaos, and Colt's shout, his final thrust and the strength with which he held himself fast and deep inside her, conveyed his pleasure.

She could feel his cock ejaculating within the thin latex sheath, and the sensation of the hot, semen-filled sac pulsing against her cervix pushed her into a second, unexpected climax.

Thank God Colt had his hands on her, she'd have collapsed otherwise.

For long moments afterward, the sound of harsh breathing punctuated by the gentle spray of the shower echoed in the glass enclosure.

"Mother of God, woman, you're going to kill me."

"Me? I've been taken over by super cock times two." Susan pushed away from the wall, straightened, and turned to face Colt. Just like a well-choreographed dance, he slipped an arm around her and pulled her in at the same time she wound her arms around his neck.

She felt him move, and the water stopped.

"I don't want to run your hot water heater dry."

"I have a really big one. We all do."

"Who's we?"

"My family. The one my fathers installed in the Big House actually puts us all to shame."

"Fathers? As in more than one male parent?"

"Mmm? Oh, yeah. They're brothers—twins, actually. Their names are Jonathan and Caleb. Retired now from ranching and law enforcement, respectively. My older brothers kind of take after them, since Steven is a rancher and Matt the deputy sheriff of Lusty. They married my best friend Kelsey a few months ago."

"But which one of them is actually your father? You can only have one."

Susan was used to getting questions about her family from her lovers, but usually it was the whole ménage relationship dynamic they questioned. She went up on her toes, kissed Colt squarely on the mouth, then stepped back.

She didn't want to examine why she'd felt compelled to mention her family. Usually, that came much later, when she had a sense of her lovers and how what she had to tell them might play.

Well, she'd opened her mouth. The only thing left to do was wrap it up and change the subject. "They're, both of them, my father. That's the Benedict way. Come on, driller-man. Somehow, I've really worked up an appetite. Let's eat."

## Chapter 7

"I usually don't do more than coffee and toast in the morning." Susan looked up from the steaming eggs on her plate to give the cook a smile. "But this omelet looks great, Ryder." Sprinkled with chunks of green pepper, mushroom, onion, and tiny pieces of ham, the omelet rivaled her mother's—or Kelsey's—breakfast offerings.

"You're out of hot sauce," Ryder said, "or this would have been perfect."

"Not for me. I've never acquired a taste for hot sauce on my eggs." She forked some of the omelet into her mouth. She hadn't noticed the cheese, and the creamy texture with the eggs was one of her favorite flavor combinations. When she opened her eyes, it was to see that both men had stilled.

They looked at her as if she'd grown two heads. "What?"

"No hot sauce on your eggs? Are you sure you're Texan?" Colt asked.

Susan grinned. "That's what my entire family says. Well, except for my new sister-in-law, Kelsey. She has the restaurant in town, and while she serves eggs with hot salsa, she doesn't eat them that way."

They sat like three points of a triangle around Susan's breakfast table. Her face colored as she recalled the other use they'd put the sturdy piece of furniture to yesterday.

"Which brother is she married to?" Ryder asked.

"Matthew and Steven. Their wedding was just a few months ago." She forked another mouthful of omelet and then casually looked up to see how that piece of information fared.

Ryder's brow was creased. "She's married to *two* of your brothers?"

"It's the Benedict way," Susan said.

"I see."

Susan could tell that he didn't really see at all, but that was all right. She thought Colt might say something then, since she'd used the same expression with him during their shower. That man, however, kept silent. Not that he didn't communicate with Ryder, but the look that passed between the two men remained a mystery to her. She didn't know if she was disappointed or not that neither men pursued the topic of "the Benedict way".

"While we're drilling your new well, what's on your agenda today?" Colt asked.

"I'd only just got started with prepping the trim for new paint when you two arrived yesterday. I need to get back to that. I want to start painting by the end of the week."

"We'll help you with the roof trim," Colt said. "It's got to be a good thirty feet off the ground, and we're used to working with heights."

"I welcome all the help I can get." Susan's mind wouldn't let her curiosity go. Why hadn't either man asked for clarification about her family? Any time she'd mentioned her family to others, she could count on varied reactions and the inevitable questions.

*Alex and Josh knew them.* Of course, that had to be it! Knowing her brothers, they also likely already knew about her family's unusual history and lifestyle.

"More coffee?"

Susan blinked. She hadn't even seen Colt pick up the pot. "Yes, please." She looked down at her plate and realized she'd finished her breakfast.

"I'm going to go grab a shower." Ryder got up from the table and dealt with his dirty dishes. "Any reason why we can't just keep our bags in your room?"

They'd not discussed the future, and really, it was too soon for that. But they did have the next few days together, and Susan could see no reason to stop sharing everything now.

"No, that'll be fine." Better than fine, if yesterday was any indication. Susan took a slow, appreciative sip of her very good coffee. She was already looking forward to when they would all quit working for the day.

* * * *

It had been a long time since he and Colt had worked, just the two of them, to bring in a well. Even though their lifestyle had improved immeasurably since those first shaky years, money really wasn't everything. He'd missed this, the sweating together to make their own way.

"Time to add another section of pipe." Colt lifted his head from looking down at where the last section of pipe entered the bore hole.

"The report said the strata weren't very thick in this area, and there could be water at a thousand feet, but I'm wondering if it's as uniform here as the geologists thought." Sometimes, Ryder knew, the science wasn't perfect.

He held the swivel still and let his thoughts wander. His gaze followed them. Susan Benedict worked with her back to them, scraping the old paint from the trim on the house.

"Hell of a woman." He turned his gaze to Colt.

"She is that. I'll make breakfast tomorrow, by the way." Colt said.

"Bet your ass you will."

Colt laughed. "Do you remember the semi-drunken conversation we had New Year's Day, after Melissa left?"

Ryder didn't miss a beat. "You mean after she tossed us aside and thanked us for the ride?"

Colt finished maneuvering fresh pipe into place. In their larger rigs, every moving part was powered by hydraulics. This baby, their original portable rig, required a lot of muscle. Ryder moved the traveling block back up while Colt finished his part. They worked in silence, both of them nodding satisfaction once the new pipe had been screwed into place.

Colt looked over at Susan and then turned his attention back to Ryder and resumed their conversation. "Yeah, after that."

"I remember we were both pissed," Ryder said, "and disappointed because, to her, it had all just been an experiment. I don't get that sense with Susan at all."

"No. Even though we're having fun and games, she's not flippant about the three of us," Colt agreed. "Do you recall what we both said we'd do if we ever found a woman capable of putting up with us both for the long term?"

"I do. Even though we neither of us truly believed we'd ever find a woman *together* enough to let us share her for the long term." They'd never, either of them, believed they'd make suitable husband material, simply because of where they'd come from. They each carried what they considered to be bad blood. Yet somehow, the idea of sharing a wife, of making a family that would be three instead of two—in essence, sharing the role of husband as they'd shared most everything else since they'd met—*that* idea had felt good and righteous to them both. "I do remember that, while I was slightly inebriated, we weren't either of us joking when we said that, between us, we'd make one pretty good husband. It's too soon to tell if that's where we're headed. I know that. But I have to admit, last New Year's is where my thoughts took me last night just before I fell asleep."

"I think we might be here for longer than a week." Colt steadied the pipe while Ryder turned the drill back on. This old rig—they'd nicknamed her Delilah—wasn't near as pretty or high tech as the other rigs they owned. But damned if she wasn't dependable and gutsy as hell.

"We've neither of us taken a vacation in a long time," Ryder said. "Our timing's off, though. We're going to be needed in Houston in a couple of weeks, and then we'll want to see the start of that co-op project we've just signed onto with Susan's brothers."

"Maybe we can get her to come with us…and maybe we should spend some time in that hometown of hers, too."

"Any particular reason for that?" Colt's suggestion came from out in left field, as far as Ryder could tell.

"It's not just her brothers who have an alternative lifestyle. The lady has two fathers. As in, her mother has two husbands. She said it was the Benedict way. Just like she told you."

"Huh. Then maybe we should find out just what the Benedict way is all about." Ryder turned to look at Susan, but she was no longer in sight. *Likely working on the other side of the house.* Chuckling, he put his attention back on the job, and the conversation. "I must admit I'm a bit curious about a town named *Lusty*."

Colt laughed. "It does conjure images."

"So does Ms. Benedict." And that, Ryder thought, was the bottom line.

* * * *

The sound of drilling settled into the background, a kind of music that kept the image of the men operating it front and center in Susan's thoughts. As she gave herself over to the mindless task of scouring the house's trim, her brain was free to dwell on the last twenty-four hours.

*I'm a coward.*

Funny, but she'd never realized that about herself before. It was the reason she'd stopped talking about her family. In the next instant, she wanted to discard the label of cowardice. Good Lord, she'd only known Colt and Ryder not even a full twenty-four hours. A little precipitous for her to be wondering what they'd make of her family, and the Benedict way.

*Not too early to let them have all kinds of freedom with your body.*

Maybe if Susan hadn't been raised with a family tradition of ménage relationships and historic cases of love at first sight, she'd be feeling guilty right about now.

*Love at first sight.* Not that she was in love with those two wildcatters. It was way too soon for that. But she'd fallen into lust at first sight, and that, in her estimation, had to be just as rare.

Besides, she'd certainly taken as many liberties with their bodies as they had with hers.

The sound of the drill stopped, and she sensed a hot gaze on her back and waited a beat. When she looked over her shoulder, both men looked busy, adding more casing pipe into the bore hole. She wondered how deep the well would end up being.

The geological report she'd received had been more than a decade old. She had no idea if it had been created with the help of the latest satellite imaging, or not.

The sun blazed down, hot for mid autumn. Using the back of her hand, she wiped the sweat from her brow and stood back to survey the job she'd done so far. Not bad, if she did say so herself.

She could easily have hired painters to do this, but doing it herself gave her enormous pleasure.

Just as the upgrades she'd done inside the house filled her with pride. Little by little, she was making this Benedict holding *her* home.

She'd done all she could prepping the exterior from the ground. It was time to go back to the other side of the house and deploy the ladder.

Though small by Benedict standards, Susan had fallen in love with this century-old ranch house the moment she'd laid eyes on it. She'd approached the town trust to ask permission to move in and take over managing the land. As a member of one of the founding families of Lusty, she could claim part ownership in every building, every acre that comprised the town and surrounding area. Any of them could use any part of the trust, with the agreement of the majority.

The only thing none of them could ever do was sell any property.

That's the way their town, their birthright, had been set up and protected more than a hundred years before by Warren Jessop, attorney-at-law.

Susan picked up the ladder she'd taken out of the barn yesterday and began to open it into full, extension ladder mode. She thought briefly of the conversation she'd had at breakfast with the wildcatters. They'd been earnest, and not just polite, when they said they'd give her a hand with the upper story and anything else she needed to do that was tricky. She figured if they were still willing tomorrow, she'd take them up on their offer of help. She wanted to be independent, but she wasn't a fool. But the drilling rig had been running steady—well, except when they stopped to add new pipe—since that morning. Colt and Ryder had their hands full at the moment with establishing her new well.

The ladder, when fully extended, stretched to forty feet, which she figured would be high enough to work on the roof trim. She figured as she got each section done, she'd move her perch, then retract it as needed.

It shouldn't take her more than a couple of good solid days of elbow grease to get the place ready for new paint.

After making certain the base of the ladder was planted solidly on the ground, she stuffed the wire brush in her pocket, held the scraper between her teeth—yuck, it tasted *terrible*—and ascended to the top of the house.

She held on to the edge of the roof as she used first the brush and then the scraper to dispense with the old layers of paint decorating the trim. Here, as below, she found both brown and a deep forest green. She shook her head. *Why is it people find it so hard to do a job properly*? Yes, it was more work and took more time to scrape off old layers of paint first, but the finished job would look so much better.

One of the first things she looked for in people when she met them was their work ethic. Her Grandma Kate was fond of saying that idle hands were the devil's tool and an idle mind, his playground. Susan smiled, thoughts of her favorite grandparent settling softly within her. Grandma Kate was forever twisting her axioms and clichés, but her versions tended to be more precise and, to Susan's mind, a lot more entertaining.

"Susie? Can you come down here, sweetheart?"

Susan looked down toward the ground in response to Colt's voice. He was giving her a big smile. She hadn't even realized the drill had stopped working, so lost had she been in her own thoughts.

Both Colt and Ryder stood at the base and on either side of the ladder, each with a hand resting on the frame of it.

"Sure. Just give me another couple of minutes. I'm almost done this section, here."

"Now, please? It's kind of important." Ryder's smile seemed every bit as engaging as Colt's.

She wondered if there had been a problem with the well, though their smiles didn't seem to suggest trouble of any sort.

"Well, all right, if it's important."

She tucked her brush in her jeans pocket and slipped the scraper between her teeth for her descent. She really ought to thinking about getting herself one of those tool belts—

"Hey!" The scraper dropped to the ground when she yelled.

Colt had plucked her off the ladder when she still had a few steps left to go. She didn't know how he managed it, but in seconds, he'd turned her around to face him without her feet once touching the ground.

The smile on his face was gone, and he looked mad as hell. His hands that grasped her arms were trembling.

"I told you we'd do the ladder work." He gave her a shake that felt far from harsh but certainly wasn't gentle. "You agreed. Damn it, woman, you didn't even have anyone spotting the fucking ladder. You could have broken your damn fool neck."

Susan's temper went from nonexistent to eruption in two seconds flat. Kicking her feet, she tried to break free of Colt's hold. "Did you just call me a fool? I'll have you know I've been looking out for myself for a long time! How dare you—"

"That was before we got here. We said we'd do it, and we meant it." He gave her another little shake, and then he more or less tossed her over his shoulder in a fireman's carry and began to walk.

"What the hell do you think you're doing? Put me down!"

"We're going to show you what happens when you disobey us."

"*Disobey you*? Who the hell are you to order me about? What are you going to do, send me to my room?"

"No, Susie Q," Ryder answered, and confirmed with his next words that he spoke for the both of them. "We're going to paddle your ass."

"That's not funny! Put me down. You can't go carting me around like this." Neither man answered her. Ryder stepped ahead and opened the back door.

"Okay, you've made your point. I'm sorry. Now put me down."

"Of course I'll put you down," Colt said. Susan noticed his tone lacked humor. "As soon as we get upstairs, I'm going to put you down right across my knee."

Short moments later, Susan discovered that Colt wasn't kidding.

## Chapter 8

Morton's hand shook as he replaced the receiver of the phone. A part of him wanted to get into his car and storm on over to the phone company, complain about their shoddy communications system, or, better, pound the living shit out of someone. The rest of him knew it wouldn't do any good, that nothing would do any good.

His home phone hadn't been damaged and didn't need repair. It had been disconnected.

"Damn it to hell!" He swept the phone off the table, hurling the device across the floor.

The special delivery letter from the bank lay unopened on his kitchen table. He'd carried it all the way to the back of the house after signing for it, tossing it on the table, and then came in here. He'd wanted to call…who? Someone. Anyone.

*It doesn't matter that the phone's dead. You've got no one left to call.*

Leaving the room that had been his home office—a once cluttered, busy space, but now, eerily nude of equipment—he ignored his father's voice and headed for the library.

Or what used to be the library. This room at one time had housed thousands of books, some of them first editions. He'd sold the books several months ago. Now, the shelves stood empty, mute testimony to his failure. They wouldn't stand there mocking him much longer, though.

He'd sold the shelves yesterday, and a man was coming to get them tomorrow.

"Time for a change. I'm a modern man. I don't need an old-fashioned library."

Fortunately, Morton still had his bar cabinet, and even more fortunately, it was still very well stocked.

He poured himself a half glass of Jack and knocked it back quickly. The burning trail down his throat to his stomach felt like a welcome friend. Standing there by the bar, he poured himself another shot, drinking it in one gulp as well. He wasn't sure why he thought about his nanny, Petra, and the way she used to make him quaff down his cold medicine when he'd been knee high to a grasshopper.

He poured a third drink, this time a deeper one. He eyed the biggest chair in the room, the leather and oak arm chair that was his father's favorite. Keeping hold of the bottle—no sense not to, he'd need a refill quick enough—he wandered over to the chair and settled himself in it.

*That's a damn fine chair. Leather from our own stock. A real man learns how to be self-sufficient, Morton.*

He could hear his father's voice, of course, but chose to ignore it. If Morton closed his eyes, he imagined he could still catch the scents he'd long before associated with his father, Cuban cigars and Courvoisier.

Morton drank deeply, not wanting to think what his father would say about his current predicament.

Not wanting to think about it didn't seem to matter. His father's spirit filled this entire house, a house Jonas Barnes inherited from *his* father. Morton was the third generation of Barnes's to occupy this place. He would also be the last. Through the haze of memory and whiskey, he could hear his father's derisive laughter.

*Didn't I tell you you'd always be a fuckup? That's your mother's side of the family coming through. I should have beaten you more often, you useless little prick.*

"I'm not a fuckup. The economy took a dump. The entire country is suffering, it's not just me. It's not my fault."

*You haven't changed. You're always making excuses. The entire country isn't suffering. Those two wildcatters you used to be hooked to are doing just fine.*

"They were nothing but thieving, conniving bastards. They took me for a ride." Barnes took another sip from his glass, then used the tumbler as a pointer. "They'd be nowhere today if they hadn't had my money and influence in the beginning. Not my fault they deceived me."

*Of course it's your fault. You're a fuckup. If you couldn't be smart enough to succeed on your own, the least you could have done was to stay latched on to those that are.*

"Those two? They're nothing but white trash. No-accounts, street urchins. That's where I made my mistake. I never should have connected with them in the first place. Not our kind at all."

*Not our kind? They're smart, they're gutsy. Maybe they're not your kind. They turned out the way I'd hoped you would have.*

"You don't know anything, Daddy. It's a different world these days. Different than when you were making your way up the ladder. You had an easy time of it. Market conditions were right, hell, they were booming. All those sweet deals just fell into your hands. It's different today."

*Not so different. There're winners and losers, like always. You're a loser, Morton. Always have been, always will be. Those two, Evans and Magee? They're real men. A man would be proud to have sons like them. I wish they'd been my boys.*

Deep inside, Morton heard his father's words echo, the familiar battering of them stirring his temper. Always before, he'd suppressed that rage, telling himself he did so out of respect for his father.

Telling himself a lie.

Deep inside, where his emotions churned, he felt something swell then break free. Rage like he'd never known consumed him, consumed him like a fire, eating his thoughts, his will, until only the bitter ash of failure remained.

"You go to hell, you old bastard! You just go to hell, you hear me?" Furious with a man who took up space only in his head, Morton heaved the crystal highball glass against the wall. The heavy crystal bounced onto the floor and rolled toward one of the bookshelves.

"Go to hell. And you can take those two pieces of trash with you." He unscrewed the bottle cap and sucked back Jack Daniels right out of the bottle. Like a real man. "I'll show you. I'll fucking show you and show them what happens when you mess with Morton Barnes."

The whole fucking world would soon know he was a man to be taken seriously.

So Morton sat back, and he drank, and he planned.

\* \* \* \*

Susan's heart thudded in her chest in almost perfect cadence to the rhythm of Colt's footsteps as he climbed the stairs to her bedroom.

"You are not going to spank me!" She'd never been spanked, not even when she was a child.

"Yes, I am."

She fought off the wave of dizziness as he lifted her off his shoulder and held her in front of him so she faced him. Her feet had barely touched the ground when she felt Ryder's hands slide around her waist from behind. He had the snap on the front of her jeans open and her zipper down in seconds.

"Do you have any idea how easy it would have been for you to fall and seriously hurt yourself?"

She stood toe to toe with Colt, and if he'd looked mean or just bossy, she'd have fought him with unwavering grit. She'd been raised by one father who'd worked in law enforcement and another who'd been a tough-as-nails rancher. She knew how to defend herself. But as she looked at Colt, and then Ryder, who'd moved to stand beside him, arms folded in front of his chest, a couple of truths hit home.

The first was that they both appeared genuinely concerned about her well-being. The second was what she should have realized first off, right away.

They'd both been scared for her.

That fact tempered her response. "I've climbed ladders before. I've even fallen off of one before."

"Key word here is 'before.'" Colt's voice softened. "That was *before* you mattered to us. We told you last night that you're ours. No one threatens what's ours, not even you."

The fervor of his declaration stunned her, so much so that she offered no resistance when he sat on the side of her bed and then grabbed her hand, drawing her forward.

In a single motion that seemed practiced, Ryder yanked her pants down and Colt pulled her over his knee.

*Smack.* Susan blinked, the surprise of the blow, of actually being spanked, a shock wave that shivered through her body.

*Smack. Smack.*

"Ouch! Damn it to hell, that hurts." Well, it didn't *just* hurt, but that was entirely beside the point.

"Really?" Ryder's one-word rejoinder made her want to laugh.

"One more," Colt said.

*Smack.* He left his hand on her bare ass, and in that moment, Susan recalled what she'd been trying to remember the night before. She remembered what her brothers had said to her when, inebriated and feeling sorry for herself, she'd confessed her fear that she'd never find the kind of men she longed for.

Manly men who'd take care of her and give her hell when she needed it.

She came back to the present when she felt her jeans being tugged off her body completely. Colt's hand still caressed her naked and heated ass. Ryder's hand soon joined it.

"My, my, it would seem the lady doesn't mind being spanked all that much." Ryder hunkered down so that his words became a gentle warm puff against her neck.

Her breathing had hitched, the same way it had the night before when they'd begun touching her, when they'd aroused her.

She was aroused now.

Susan felt very conscious of being half naked on Colt's lap. She turned her head to look at Ryder. He leaned over and captured her lips with his own. He used one hand to help support her head while the other stayed caressing one ass cheek.

When he drew back, she said, "No, I didn't mind it all that much. And I am sorry I scared you. Both of you. I just didn't think."

"You've been running wild for quite some time, I imagine, without anyone to answer to. It'll take you a bit of time to get used to having us in that role." Colt's tone told her his mind wasn't so much on the conversation as it was on her naked bottom.

She wondered how distracted he really was. "That sounds suspiciously like a future."

"Yeah." He pulled her up so that she sat on his lap. She slipped one arm around his neck and reached for Ryder with the other hand. He brought that hand to his lips and kissed it.

Colt began to unfasten the buttons of her blouse. "Surprises the hell out of both Ryder and me that we're thinking of a future. Neither of us is one hundred percent sure what that means yet or what we will end up doing about it. So let's take things one day at a time."

"I'm all for that. One day at a time works for me, too." She let her arms fall to her sides so the men could finish undressing her. "You guys arrived when I least expected you."

"Good thing we're all on the same page, then." Ryder got to his feet. "Susan?"

She turned her attention to Ryder, who began to open his shirt. "Yes, Ryder?"

"Colt and I will finish the high work for you. Tomorrow. Okay?"

She understood the implication. There'd be no more work done today as they all had something more fun in mind. Since that was fine with her, she nodded. Then she asked, "Does that mean you found water?"

"Not yet." Colt stroked his hand back and forth under her breast. "We haven't drilled that deep yet."

Susan grinned. "Sure you have."

Colt's lips twitched in a smile as he continued to stroke her breasts. "We can multitask."

"Thank God." Susan shivered as her nipples puckered tightly. Ryder continued to shed his clothes. Because she was an equal opportunity kind of woman, she decided to get to work on the buttons of Colt's shirt. It was hard, though, to keep the thread of their conversation. "Okay, you can do the high work. Tomorrow."

Colt reached up and stroked her chin, then turned her face into his kiss. His flavor aroused her, making her open wide to him. She sucked his tongue into her mouth, stroked it with her own. Images of cock, of having one—his or Ryder's—in her mouth and sucking it in exactly the same way caused her slit to gush.

Ryder took her hand, kissed it, and brought it to his cock. Her fingers wrapped around him, and because the image had just been in her thoughts, she gently pulled her lips from Colt's and moved her mouth to Ryder's cock.

She loved the slide of him moving into her mouth. The salty heat met a need she'd only just discovered. The way he combed his fingers through her hair and then gripped her head thrilled her. She pulled her mouth almost off him, then took him in again, and then again, in a rhythm she deliberately kept languid.

Out of the corner of her eye, she could see Colt watching, his eyes riveted on the way she sucked his partner's cock. His one hand stroked up and down her back while the other continued to pet and cup her breasts.

Ryder groaned and began to gently pump his hips, letting her know how aroused he'd become. "You have a fucking *wonderful* mouth."

Unable to speak, she instead responded by cupping his scrotum and, her touch delicate, squeezing him.

"Fuck, *yes*." Ryder's hands trembled where he held her head, and the rhythm of his hips, as he fucked her mouth, increased in tempo.

Colt's hand left her breast and stroked her thighs. He exerted a light pressure, indicating he wanted her to part her legs.

She did and then moaned when his fingers sought out her slit. Up and down, he stroked her, using the same cadence his friend used to move his cock in and out of her mouth, and Susan lost herself in the heady sexual play of them both.

"I'm close. Suck, baby. Make me come." Ryder's cock twitched in her mouth, giving truth to his words. She drew on him with a steady suction. Ryder shouted as she pulled his seed from him. When she swallowed Ryder's first spurt, Colt inserted two fingers into her pussy and rubbed her clit with his thumb.

She'd been aroused, nicely so, but Colt's intimate invasion catapulted her to instant orgasm. Moaning around a mouthful of cock, Susan rode the exciting wave, the spasms of rapture sharp and long. She could feel her juices running out of her cunt as her uterus contracted, her clit vibrated with rapture, and her G-spot tried to wrap itself around the fingers teasing it.

Her climax ebbed, and she realized Ryder's hands had gone from a firm grasp of her head to a tender stroke of her hair. He gently moved his hips back just enough, and she released him but kept her head on his belly while her heart slowed. She shivered, an aftershock from her climax.

Colt chuckled. "After you come, your nipples turn as hard as diamonds."

"Only if it's a real good orgasm." Susan sighed and lifted her head from Ryder, straightening on Colt's lap. She turned toward Colt and licked his lips. Then she grinned.

"It's happened every time," Colt said.

"Like I said, if it's a real good one."

She squeaked when Ryder bent over and picked her up off Colt's lap. They were both incredibly strong, these wildcatters, and they both seemed to like to just scoop her up whenever the impulse struck them.

A woman could get used to being treated this way.

"Let's get horizontal." Ryder laid her down on the bed. He followed her down, stretching out on her left.

She turned her attention to Colt, standing beside the bed, stripping out of the rest of his clothes. "I hope you're going to make my nipples go hard again."

He smiled and reached into the nightstand drawer. He withdrew the box of condoms, opened it, and upended the contents onto the table. "Sweetheart, they're going to be so hard you'll scream."

Another afternoon and evening spent having hot monkey sex. "Oh, goody."

Susan made a note to pick up some high-energy snack bars the next time she went into Lusty. At this rate, they were all going to need them.

## Chapter 9

"Welcome to Lusty, Texas." Susan announced.

"You love this place," Ryder said.

"It's home." Her tone said it all.

Lusty, Texas, featured one stoplight, smack-dab in the middle of town. Colt let his eyes wander as he waited for that light to change. To his left, three people strolled along—a woman with two men on either side of her—hand in hand in hand. He saw another trio on the other side of the street, walking, laughing, and yes, holding hands. He shot a glance at Ryder to see if he'd noticed.

"Maybe it's something in the water," Ryder said.

Susan laughed. "No, it's just Lusty."

"It certainly is," Ryder said.

Up ahead on the left, he could see a hardware store, a bank, a museum, and the restaurant—Lusty Appetites—run by Susan's new sister-in-law.

They'd just passed the sheriff's office, and he'd bet he'd personally encounter someone in uniform before they got too much further along. On his right, he'd passed a grocery, a shoe store, the fire house, and a clinic. Across from the restaurant stood a convenience store and a pharmacy.

There weren't a lot of people on the street this Saturday near the noon hour, but there were some, and every one of them turned to give his aging Ford and them a good look-see.

Frowns turned to smiles and waves when they saw Susan tucked in between him and Ryder.

"How about lunch and then the hardware store?" Susan looked from him to Ryder. "We seem to keep skipping our evening meal."

"We all ate last night," Ryder said in that slow drawl he liked to use. "Just wasn't food."

Colt couldn't keep from smiling at the sound of Susan's laughter.

"Lunch first sounds like a good idea," Colt said. "Give your sister-in-law the chef and your brother the deputy sheriff time to check us out."

"No one's going to 'check you out.'" Susan's announcement came with a token punch to his shoulder. "This is a small town and, yes, my hometown, but trust me. My family has faith in me and my judgment completely."

There was a parking spot right in front of the pharmacy, so Colt grabbed it. Once he'd turned off the engine and pocketed the keys, he turned to Susan. "After what you told us happened a few months ago to your sister-in-law, I'd be sorely disappointed if the folks in this town *didn't* check us out."

Her smile faded, chased away by a shiver. "That was horrible. Every time I think of Kelsey running down the road away from that bastard…it all could have ended so, so differently."

"Hey." Colt slipped his arm around her and gave her a hug. "Evans and Magee's number one rule of survival is to never dwell on what might have been."

"Damn straight," Ryder said. "Things more or less work out the way they're meant to be, to my way of thinking. As scary as that was for y'all, things ended up right in the end. Now let's go eat."

"Ryder Magee, you've got the soul of a poet!"

Colt grinned because Susan Benedict wasn't the first woman to say words to that effect to his best friend. She was, however, the first one to say them and make the big man blush.

"Nah, I'm just a Texan boy, bred and born." Ryder opened the door and exited the truck, repositioning his Stetson on his head and adjusting his sunglasses—actions Colt knew he used as a personal sort of time-out.

Colt checked his side mirror for traffic then opened his door and pressed the lock button before closing it again.

"This is Lusty. You don't have to lock your truck." Susan's faith in her town carried the ring of truth.

Colt could have pointed out to her that Lusty wasn't a gated community. Hell, they currently had a couple of down and dirty wildcatters in their midst, proving the place was open to all kinds of unsavory types. But Susan's selective naïveté was refreshing. A part of him hoped she never lost it.

Ryder reached the door of the restaurant first and held it open for them.

Inside the eatery, the aroma of fresh baked bread and spicy barbeque sauce teased his nose and made his tummy rumble. Susan hadn't been kidding about skipping the evening meals over the last few days. Now, the smell of good food reminded his stomach how empty it had been of late.

"Smells good in here," Ryder said.

"Kelsey is a fabulous cook." Susan led them toward an empty table in the corner. A waitress made a beeline for them, and Susan stopped to greet her.

"Hi, Ginny. How are you? And how's Benny doing?"

At first glance, the waitress—Ginny—didn't look to be much older than a teenager. Her long brown hair had been caught up in a ponytail, and when she'd jogged over to meet them, it had swung behind her, reinforcing the young image.

Then Colt looked into her eyes. The woman flinched away from his direct gaze, but he'd glimpsed an old soul before she did.

"I'm great, thanks. And Benny got two A's on his last report card!"

"Wow, good for him! You must be so proud."

"I sure am. We came straight here so he could show Kelsey and Matt, and then we had apple pie and ice cream to celebrate."

Susan looked toward the table she'd been leading them to. Ginny reached out and lightly touched her arm.

"Kelsey said to seat y'all at number eight and to tell you you're having the lunch special today."

Colt wondered at the expression that crossed Susan's face for just a moment. Then his woman smiled, and he forgot his next thought.

"Reckon Colt had it right," Ryder said as he held Susan's chair for her.

Colt counted the place settings at the large round table. "Your sister-in-law, your brother the deputy, and one more person will be joining us, by the look of things."

Susan shook her head. "Likely Steven, my other brother." She kept her gaze on the table as if counting the number of places for herself. Then she looked up at him and Ryder. "I'm sorry about this. I thought it would be a good idea to just grab something to eat here before picking up my paint over at the hardware store."

"I've got no problems being interrogated by a deputy sheriff," Colt said.

"Unless he brings out the rubber hoses," Ryder added.

Susan shot Ryder and him an annoyed look. "Nobody is going to interrogate you!" she said.

Some minutes later, Colt wondered if perhaps he should have bet her on that one.

First, they were greeted by Kelsey Benedict, who seemed too petite and dainty to run a full-service restaurant and balance two husbands. Looks, Colt reminded himself, were often deceiving.

From the moment the petite, green-eyed brunette joined them at the table, Colt felt as if he'd been very deftly "managed".

Susan had, of course, gotten to her feet to give her sister-in-law, who also happened to be her best friend, a big hug. When she sat again, it was where Kelsey had maneuvered her to, in a seat away from both Colt and Ryder. Moments later the door opened wide to admit a strapping blond man dressed in a light brown sheriff's department uniform. A lighter blond than his sister, his blue eyes focused on him and Ryder as if they were on the FBI's ten most wanted list. Matthew Benedict kissed his wife, then his sister, and sat at the table, smack-dab in front of Colt, and beside Susan.

"Gentlemen," was his only word of greeting.

"What a surprise." Susan's voice belied that statement, and Colt tried not to laugh when she scowled at her brother.

"If my arrival surprised you, you're about to be absolutely astounded."

Matthew had no sooner said that when the door to the street opened once more, admitting a man who, but for his dark hair and eyes, could have been Matthew's twin.

Dressed in jeans and a tee, this man also kissed Kelsey, then Susan, and sat in the remaining chair, beside Kelsey.

Colt approved the tactic of the brothers Benedict sandwiching the two women between them.

"I had no idea we were going to be treated to a family luncheon," Susan said. She glared at both brothers.

Because she'd not done the honors as she had with Kelsey, Colt introduced himself and Ryder.

"Josh and Alex sent them to me," Susan said.

One look at her face and he knew she was ticked. "Susan." Colt could appreciate her rancor, and knew it was in part fueled by embarrassment. "It's all right, sweetheart. Your brothers have every right to insist on meeting us."

Her response was to give him a smile that made him wish they were all three back at her place.

He switched his gaze from her to Matthew, only to find that man regarding his sister, a thoughtful expression on his face.

"So you know Alex and Josh," Steven said.

Ginny brought over a tray of drinks—tea for everyone but Kelsey, who'd asked for water. Colt waited until the young woman had set down the glasses.

"We've known them for a couple of years, as we tend to bump elbows at the same gatherings in Houston. As of last week, however, we became business partners."

Matthew tilted his head to one side. "You're the wildcatters they were talking about taking on as partners in the Evercroft deal?" He half closed his eyes, and Colt knew he was searching his memory. "*Dos Hombres*? The small outfit started up from out of El Paso?"

Because he'd made the words "small outfit" sound like something he didn't want to step in, Colt said, "Not that small, thank you very much. And yes, that's us. After we shook on the deal, your brothers asked us if we could do them a favor and drill a new water well for your sister on her ranch. Since it had been a while since we'd had the opportunity to handle the equipment ourselves—our first love—we jumped at the chance." Only after the words had escaped his lips did Colt realize they could be taken two ways. Fortunately, another matter claimed the Benedicts' attention.

"Damn it, Susie, are you still living off in the middle of nowhere on that piece of scrub land laughingly called a ranch?" Steven seemed really aggrieved.

Before Susan could say anything, his wife did. "Susan likes that ranch, and she has a perfect right to be there if that's where she wants to be."

"I can speak for myself, Kels." Susan reached over and squeezed her friend's hand.

"I know that. It's just that your brothers are being particularly pigheaded all of a sudden, and I, for one, don't like it. I'm not very happy with your attempted heavy-handedness, either one of you."

"Uh-oh." Matthew looked over at his brother, one eyebrow raised. "You remember what the dads always say."

Steven nodded. "Yep. If the woman of the house isn't happy, no one's going to be happy."

Colt thought it had to be a measure of comfort on their part that the brothers would talk so openly about family.

"It's all right, Mrs. Benedict." Ryder leaned forward and directed his comments to Kelsey. "Like Colt said, we've no problem being scrutinized by Susan's family."

Ginny returned with a tray that seemed bigger than she was. Loaded onto it were plates piled high with food that smelled heavenly.

"Looks good." One of Colt's personal favorites was chopped steak. This one came smothered with cooked onions and mushrooms and—he inhaled deeply—jack cheese. Steak cut fries had been heaped on the side with thick gravy, and Colt knew he was in for a treat.

Knowing it was rude not to wait, and not caring, he picked up his fork and cut into the meat.

"My God." Ryder's exclamation told him he wasn't alone in his haste.

Colt chewed slowly to give his stomach a chance to prepare for the feast. "Damn, that's good."

"You look as if you've not seen a decent meal in ages. Isn't Susie feeding you?" Matthew asked.

Colt froze, his gaze going directly to Susan. He had to strangle back a laugh because his woman's face had gone totally red. He flicked a glance at Ryder and knew his friend wasn't doing much better hanging on to his composure. Then he caught the incredulous stare Kelsey shot her husband.

"Um…why don't we forget I just said that?"

"Do you think?" Susan asked.

Kelsey seemed determined to change the subject because she looked down at her plate. She speared a French fry with her fork.

"Had some Canadian tourists in here the other day. Do you know they put *vinegar* on their fries?"

"I heard that," Ryder said.

Everyone seemed fascinated with their lunch. Colt took another couple of bites and decided that Kelsey Benedict did have a talent in the kitchen.

"So, what have you been up to?" Steven asked of Susan, and Colt closed his eyes and shook his head. Was there any hope for this conversation?

"The roof line of her house, but that isn't going to happen again anytime soon." He knew Susan wouldn't appreciate being put on the spot, but he thought the faster they steered away from double entendre hell, the better.

"Our sister does tend to want to try and do every damn thing herself," Steven said. Colt thought he might always have that ruddy complexion.

"I'm right here, you moron. Why did I ever think the two of you were my favorite brothers?"

Colt wondered if all-out sibling war was imminent. The words "saved by the bell" came to mind when he heard the ringing of a cell phone. Until he realized the phone that was ringing was his.

He pulled the device out of his pocket and looked at the display. "Huh. Our office admin." He and Ryder had both left instructions they were only to be called in the case of an emergency. His gut knotted. "Excuse me, please, while I take this." He flipped open the phone. "Evans."

"Colt? We have a problem." His usually unflappable admin, Nancy, sounded scared. He shot a look at Ryder, who set down his fork, immediately alert.

"What kind of problem?"

"There's been an explosion at the site of the number two rig. Colt, Murphy's hurt. He's hurt bad."

## Chapter 10

Susan hated the smell of hospitals. She didn't know why, but there it was. Usually she only set foot in one under the most dire of circumstances.

One look at both Colt and Ryder's expressions when they'd heard about the explosion and she knew there was no place she'd rather be than with them.

"Have you known him a long time?" She sat beside Ryder in the waiting room as they awaited news. Their friend and employee, Michael Murphy, was in surgery and had been since they'd arrived at the hospital in San Angelo. The men handled anxiety differently. Colt paced, Ryder hunkered down. *Funny, I'd have thought they'd do the opposite.*

"Yeah. As an employee, he's been with us since the beginning." Ryder huffed out a breath and sat back against the chair. She'd kept her hand on his leg, and now, he picked it up, threaded his fingers through hers. "I should say our *second* beginning. Actually, he's the father neither of us ever had."

Coldplay's *Viva La Vida* began to play. Colt stopped in his pacing, pulled his cell phone out of his pocket. "Evans."

Ryder's focus shifted to his partner. Susan wondered if the call was from Matthew. She'd been pleased her brother had volunteered to accompany them to the drill site—a private field outside San Angelo. When it became clear her men needed to get to the hospital, to be there for their friend, Matt had volunteered to stay behind and act as a liaison between them and the investigators.

No question the site had been crawling with cops and emergency personnel from the moment the explosion occurred.

Colt's expression turned hard, and Ryder's body tensed next to hers.

"Son of a bitch. I knew it had to be something like that. Murph—" His voice caught, and he closed his eyes. Susan already knew him well enough to understand he had to reach deep to suppress the emotion running through him.

He cared so much about her after such a short time together. How much more would he care for a man he considered his father?

"Murphy's middle name is 'safety,'" Colt continued. Then he listened, nodding his head. "If you could, I'd appreciate it. Thanks, Benedict. I owe you one."

"Sabotage?" Ryder's one word sent a chill down Susan's spine.

"Looks like. The investigation is still in the early stages, but one of the firemen combing the scene found evidence of an explosive device. From what they see so far, they think it was set to go at a specific time, and it was right there in the manager's trailer."

"A bomb? Someone set a *bomb* at your work site?" Outrage warred with fear inside her. Ryder held her hand tighter, and Colt squatted in front of her.

"That's what it looks like. Matt said the fire department investigators were notifying federal authorities."

"Who would do such a thing?" She wanted to ask other questions but didn't. She wondered if their company had been the target or if Mr. Murphy had been the intended victim of the blast.

Colt stroked her cheek, bringing her gaze back to him.

"That's the question, and until we have some answers, I think it would be a good idea if you went home."

Everything inside Susan went still. "I beg your pardon?"

The men proved they were adept at reading her mood. She could tell they knew she was pissed by the look that passed between them and the gentleness with which they each touched her.

"Sweetheart, we were supposed to be there today, the both of us. We changed our plans a couple of days ago—more or less at the last minute—and sent Mike in our place."

"I'm sorry your friend has been hurt. But you don't have to feel guilty about that. It's not your fault. It's the fault of whoever did this. Sending me away might feel like a just penance, but..."

"Susan." Ryder squeezed her hand. "Sweetheart, we're not asking you to go home as penance, and certainly *not* because we want to be without you."

Then she got it. She shook her head, because usually, she wasn't quite that slow. "You're sending me away because you think someone's out to get you—the two of you."

"Damn right. There's no way in hell we'll tolerate your being in the line of fire." Colt's voice was as hard as she'd ever heard it. "There is no doubt at all. That trailer is where we go each morning at the start of the day, where we go over whatever analysis came in overnight, where we have our first cup of joe and set the game plan for the day."

"And you think it would be a good idea for me to disappear? I'm not some delicate miss to be set off to the side just because there might be danger about." She folded her arms and gave them each a good stare so they would know she was serious.

"There's no 'might' about it," Colt said. "Most people tend to agree bombs are dangerous. It appears that Ryder and I have an enemy. An unseen, unknown enemy. The first thing we need to do is take you someplace where you'll be safe."

"Well, then, wildcatter, we have a problem because there is no way in hell I'm leaving either one of you. I'm here. I'm staying. Deal with it."

"God damn it." Colt got to his feet and likely would have given her a blast if the door to the waiting room hadn't opened just then.

Colt spun on his heels, and Ryder got to his feet as the man dressed in green scrubs entered the room.

"Are you folks here for Mr. Murphy?"

"Yes," Colt and Ryder said at the same time.

Because her men went over to the doctor, Susan went to them, stood between them, and put a hand on each of their backs. Both men shook, the tremors likely not visible to the doctor, but she felt them, and she understood them.

"I'm Doctor Scott. Mr. Murphy is a lucky man. He came through the surgery and is in recovery."

"Thank God." Colt's words emerged on a heavy sigh. She felt both of her lovers exhale with relief. She stayed silent and focused on just being there for them.

"The surgery was complicated, but for his age, he's in good shape, and that helped. We had to remove his spleen. Additionally, we inserted a metal plate in his left leg—it was a very bad break. He also suffered a concussion in the blast, but he was responsive prior to surgery. I'm going to take the precaution of moving him into Intensive Care for twenty-four hours, once he comes out of recovery. We want to make certain that concussion was a minor one."

"Anything Mike needs, he gets," Ryder said.

"Does Mr. Murphy have any family?" Dr. Scott asked.

"He only has us," Colt said. "When can we see him?"

"I'll have someone come and get you once he's settled in ICU," Dr. Scott said. "You'll only be able to see him for a few minutes. The nurses will explain visitation procedures to you."

"Thank you, Dr. Scott." Ryder extended his hand. "Mike means a lot to us both."

"You're welcome."

The doctor left, and both men turned and hung on to her for a moment, saying nothing. When they straightened, she wasn't surprised to see both of them had damp eyes. Colt and Ryder were as macho as they came, but they had both shown themselves capable of real caring and real emotion. Whoever said real men don't cry didn't know any real men.

"I'll give Nancy a call in a minute so she can get the word out," Ryder said.

"Good thinking." Colt ran a hand through his hair. "I guess we should see about getting a room. We'll want to stick around for a couple of days, make sure Mike is going to be okay, has everything he needs. Plus, the investigators are going to want to talk to us."

"That's already been taken care of. When I gave Kelsey an update an hour ago, I asked her to get us a room. We're at the Governor's Inn. That's we, Mr. Evans. I'm not going anywhere."

"Is that a fact?"

Something about the way Colt's voice dipped when he got serious sent shivers through her, and not the bad kind of shivers, either.

"That's a fact. I know that doesn't make you happy. But I'm a Benedict, and Benedicts don't hide, and we don't run from trouble." She stopped because there was so much she wanted to say to these men. So many things these two wildcatters made her feel, emotions she'd never felt before. Right now, first and foremost, was a fierce need to be with them, to be there *for* them. She had fallen in love with them both, and fallen fast. It wasn't time to tell them that, though. She moved so she could turn and look at them both, speak to them both. "You have to know I'll do anything you want, anything you ask. Except leave you. Please don't ask me to do that."

Colt and Ryder stared at each other for a long moment. Then they both looked at her.

"All right," Colt said. "But if it looks like all hell is going to break loose, we'll get you out of harm's way if we have to lasso you to do it. Make no mistake." He stepped forward, put his hands on her arms, and lifted her just enough to make his point. "We'll do whatever we have to do to keep you safe."

Susan carefully schooled her expression. Gloating wouldn't go over well at the moment, and she felt pretty certain a whoop of glee wouldn't be welcome, either. Neither would telling these two macho hombres that she'd been champion calf roper three years running back in the day.

She could finesse a good piece of rope with the best of them and would do whatever she had to do to keep *them* safe.

\* \* \* \*

Kelsey had booked them the penthouse suite at the Governor's Inn. Neither big nor splashy like some of the more well-known hotels, the Inn nevertheless featured top rate, luxurious accommodation geared to the busy and discriminating executive.

"Not as big as your bed," Ryder said when he opened the door to the bedroom. Then he laughed. "I never thought I'd see the day when I considered a king-sized bed too small."

Susan grinned. "When we get back to Lusty, we'll stop in at the ranch just outside town, where my brothers and Kelsey live. Their bed is even bigger than mine."

Ryder turned to face her, and Susan read the heat in his expression. He trailed his gaze down her body, instantly lighting her fires. She felt naked and raring to go. Colt came up behind her and put his hands on her shoulders. "I'm glad you're here. I need you tonight. We both need you tonight."

"I need you, too. I need you both."

How could they have come to mean so much to her so soon? She'd known the touch of other men, but only these men possessed the touch that enthralled her completely. She'd shared herself before, but with these men, she felt as if she wasn't sharing herself so much as finally becoming whole, complete.

"You look at me like that and everything inside me turns right. We're in a hell of a mess, the one person who's always been as important to me as Colt is in the hospital, yet you're here, and somehow, I know everything's going to be all right." Ryder's words kissed her skin even as Colt's hands gently caressed up and down her arms.

"I never doubted my strength," Colt said, his lips skimming her ear. "I've always been able to do what needed doing. But with you here, Susan, I feel damn near invincible."

"You complete us, when neither of us realized we'd been incomplete." Ryder said the words simply, yet Susan knew there was nothing simple about it. And weren't their words an echo of the same sense of rightness she herself felt?

She'd oh-so-boldly declared that Benedicts didn't hide, and she meant those words. But wasn't she hiding, even now? Hiding her emotions from these men in the lust and the attraction between them. Hiding from being the first one to say the words because a part of her was afraid they'd throw them back at her. The other few relationships she'd experienced really had been nothing compared to this. This was real. This was it, her one and only.

"I love you." Oh, God, totally scary stuff, especially when Ryder's eyes widened and Colt's hands squeezed her arms. "I love you both. And I've…I've never said those words to any man before."

"Thank God." Ryder cupped her face, bent to her, and laid his lips on hers. Hot and wet, deep and dangerous, he kissed her, his tongue claiming her mouth, coaxing hers into a tango as passionate as any ever danced.

Colt's hand stroked her hair, and when Ryder broke their kiss, that hand gripped her head, maneuvered her so that his mouth hovered just inches from hers. He kissed her, lightly, reverently, and Susan felt tears sting the backs of her eyes.

"I love you, Susan Benedict," Colt said. "I didn't expect to ever fall in love. Not all the way in love, not like this."

"I love you, Susie Q." Ryder's voice shook with his declaration. "I didn't even know I could love, until you came along."

"Please." She nestled her head back against Colt and reached for Ryder with her right hand, pulling him closer. "Please, show me. I need for us to be together. I need for us to be *one*."

"Don't beg, baby." Ryder leaned forward, this kiss as gentle as the one Colt had given her. "You're everything. Absolutely everything."

They moved as one, these two men she loved. Together, they freed her body from the confinement of her clothes, freed her and began to worship her. Their hands caressed her, their lips adored her, and for the first time in her life, Susan felt cherished.

*You're everything.*

She'd never been everything to anyone before, but she understood the concept very well because Colt and Ryder had somehow become everything to her.

She needed more. Reaching out, she began to open the buttons of Ryder's shirt. No longer content to just take, she wanted to give. With each new inch of flesh she uncovered, her need grew.

Ryder took over for her, stripping off the fabric that hid his body from her. She felt the movements behind her and knew Colt shed his clothing, too.

Her hands trembled, two hands she used on two men as she touched, as she caressed and petted. Fisting them, she squeezed and stroked, loving the hot-velvet-over-steel feel of their cocks.

Determined to give as well, they continued their passionate assault on her senses, hands and fingers claiming her as their own, lips stealing kisses and nibbles and sips.

Susan dropped to her knees between them. Famished for the feel and the flavor of them, using her hands and her mouth, she stroked and licked, enveloped and sucked, first one, and then the other. Back and forth, eyes closed as she relished their unique tastes, she gave and gave until their hands rested on her head and their breathing hitched.

"Enough!" Colt's one word echoed with arousal, with a will exerted to the max. The men moved as one, releasing themselves from her grip and her ardor. And then she was in Colt's arms, surrounded by his heat as he carried her the few short feet to the bed.

She wrapped herself around him as if her body could draw sustenance just from this, just from the incredible sensation of flesh against flesh. She mated her mouth to his, ravenous to drink him into herself, desperate for the communion of lips and tongue.

Colt took over the kiss, taking her deeper, dominating her in a way that answered every wish she'd ever held dear, every fantasy she'd ever imagined alone and in the dark of night.

He combed his fingers through her hair, tilted her head back just enough that their mouths parted and their gazes met.

"Take him, sweetheart. Take Ryder's cock into that wonderful cunt of yours. Then I'm going to fuck your ass. That's what you want, isn't it? You said you wanted us to be one. You want us both inside you at the same time."

"*Yes.*" It was exactly what she wanted and needed.

"Come here, woman." Ryder waited for her on the bed, stretched out on his back, one hand fisting his latex-covered cock, stroking it slowly. Her gaze took in the open bag on the floor, the clothes spilled out of it, and the condoms and lube on the bedside table.

She hadn't even heard him rummaging around, hadn't even heard him prepare himself for her.

"Come here, Susan." Ryder's voice caressed her, a lure she would not resist. "Come and impale yourself on my cock."

"God, *yes.*"

Colt set her on the edge of the bed, and she crawled up toward Ryder. Straddling him, she looked over her shoulder at Colt.

"Come on, wildcatter. I need your cock in my ass."

## Chapter 11

The expression of need on Susan's face humbled him.

Ryder reached for her, his hands finding the perfect place on her hips to lift her. He watched as her one slender, feminine hand reached down, grasped his cock, and positioned it just at the opening to her cunt.

He could swear his dick sensed her, for a surge of pure lust shot through him.

Then she began to lower herself onto him, and Ryder closed his eyes to savor the slick glide to heaven.

"Your cunt is hot and tight and wet around me, Susie Q. I love the feeling of being inside of you."

"Ryder." She lifted herself just slightly, then slid down on him again. She shivered, as if the sensation of his cock moving inside her caressed all of her nerve endings at once.

That's exactly how she felt to him.

"Fuck me, sweetheart. Pleasure us both."

Susie's smile added fuel to his fire, the sexy siren grin promising him every delight he could ever imagine. She braced her hands on his chest, smoothing them over his nipples, caressing his pecs. *What an excellent idea.* She lifted herself, the action slow and sweet, then lowered onto his cock again. He felt the clamp of her feminine muscles, a seductive stroke his cock appreciated, as it gave an answering pulse. At that moment, he felt connected to her as he'd felt connected to no other woman before.

Mimicking her, his hands found her breasts, the lush, full globes fitting into his palms perfectly. He caressed her, maneuvering his hand so that her nipples, pink and turgid, fit into the space between his thumb and forefinger.

He stretched up and treated first one, then the other of those pretty little buds to a long, lavish lick.

"Mmm. You feel so good inside me, and I love having my nipples licked and sucked."

It was on the tip of Ryder's tongue to tell her he'd love to see her nursing their child there. He flicked his gaze up and connected with Colt's. Yeah, his best friend was thinking the same thing.

"You joining the party?"

"In a minute. It totally turns me on to watch her ride you." Colt's voice sounded strained. His friend was sporting one hell of a hard-on.

"I know." Ryder shot Colt a smile. "It's the same for me, watching the two of you." He didn't know if he could explain to another human being about this connection he had with Colt.

He caught Susan's gaze, full of tenderness and understanding, and had to swallow past the lump in his throat.

"You're closer than brothers, the two of you," she said softly. "You have to be for us, the three of us, to work."

"When there was no one else," Colt said, his voice quiet, "and I had run away from home when I was eleven, I ran into Ry. From that moment, we've been each other's family."

"No one else wanted us. But we had each other, and that was enough." He didn't mind the tears shimmering in Susan's eyes. He'd never considered himself to be the sensitive sort, but he felt the emotion between them, felt the weight of it. He thought that, in years to come, he'd remember this day, this moment.

"I want you. I want you both."

"Oh, sweetheart, we know you do. You're a miracle." Ryder figured she had to be, there could be no other explanation as to why they fit so perfectly together.

"You're about to have us both. Are you ready for my cock inside your ass, baby?" Colt ran his hand down her back, and Ryder could see her melt. She was so responsive to them both. Nothing would ever match the magic the three of them made together.

"Yes, fuck me. I want to be so full of you both that I won't be able to tell where you end and I begin."

Ryder slid his hands from her breasts, around to her back. He urged her down. "Lay your head on my chest, sweetheart, and give Colt that pretty ass of yours."

\* \* \* \*

Susan shivered with delight as she leaned forward and laid her head on Ryder's chest. His heart beat steady and strong, if a little fast, and the sound of it echoed inside her. In that moment, it felt as if his heart beat in perfect cadence with her own.

Colt stroked his hand over her ass, and the thrill of his touch sent her higher. Already incredibly aroused, she wondered how much higher she could climb before exploding.

"Cold." The one-word warning came a bare second before he brushed her anus with his fingers, covered in lube. Back and forth, he spread the silky substance. That alone was an erotic element, another layer adding to her excitement. Susan shivered and clenched her inner muscles. Ryder responded by thrusting his cock up into her even deeper.

She hummed in pleasure when Colt pushed first one, and then a second finger, into her anus, testing her readiness. In her pussy, Ryder's cock pulsed heavily, as if he too could feel Colt's fingers and was responding to them.

Susan's heart began to thud heavily when Colt eased his fingers out of her. She sensed him move in behind her, she felt him kneel on the bed behind her. The heat from his body warmed her back and ass, and then, just ever so softly, he caressed her anus with his latex-covered cock.

"Oh, yes, please." Her slit released more moisture as her inner muscles shivered around Ryder's cock.

"She's incredibly turned on by the thought of your cock in her ass," Ryder said quietly.

"She's not the only one." Colt's voice sounded strained. Susan realized he must be at the very edge of his control.

He tented her and brought his cock against her anal opening. Leaning down just a bit more, Susan consciously relaxed her hips and legs, laying herself completely open to Colt, surrendering herself to whatever he wanted to do to her.

"That's sexy as hell, Susan, that kind of trust. Hang on, baby. I'm going to take you now."

She loved the way he said that, and the way he gripped her ass, spread her cheeks. She felt the heat of his cock, the head of it pressing tightly against her anus. The force of him there, of his cock opening her, created a delicious burn that she could feel all the way to her clit.

"Oh, yes, *more.*" Nothing had ever felt like this. Colt didn't hesitate, though she knew he was being careful. But he took her, his cock hot and hard and eager. He pressed into her, and once the head of his cock had breached her sphincter, he continued his entry with a slow, steady push.

"My God, Colt. Her cunt just got tighter and hotter." Ryder gave an answering thrust, a measured roll of his hips, surging his cock into her pussy so that he hit her cervix.

"Christ, Ryder, I felt that." Colt didn't sound as if he minded so much, either.

"I feel so full of you both, it's wonderful. I need more. Move, move, oh, God, *fuck* me." Susan hovered at the very edge of her climax, every nerve ending in her body seeming to come alive now that she had both cocks inside her. Her breasts shivered, and her clit tingled, and she wanted more of these fabulous sensations. She didn't want to come yet. She wanted to gorge herself on the headiness of being so full, of having both of her lovers a part of her body. She wanted to hang on tight to this apex of arousal, to keep the tingling, sizzling *almost* right there for as long as she possibly could.

"Yeah, we're going to fuck you. We're going to fuck you so fucking much you won't be able to walk after."

Colt's impassioned words made her want to giggle, except she knew how he felt. Balancing on the edge of a razor would be easier than keeping this slow and easy pace. Yet he'd leashed his needs, his desire to plunder, for her.

"Give it to me." She raised her head off Ryder, looked over her shoulder. "You won't hurt me. Give it all to me."

"Jesus, woman." Colt closed his eyes, and Susan could see the battle he waged. Both men held on to their passion with iron fists. More than anything, she needed to give them ultimate satisfaction. She wanted, needed, to give them the ultimate gift, the freedom to sate themselves in her body, to take it all. On the edge, greedy, she pushed down and then back, a dipping, rolling thrust that took both cocks deeper, giving them just that final bit of angle.

"God!" Colt thrust into her, hard and fast, at the same time Ryder levered up. They all three connected, together stroked that one sweet spot that shattered control and turned them into feral, physical beings.

"Yes!" Susan's orgasm erupted, a sharp, white comet of rapturous pleasure. Pulse after pulse of pure ecstasy poured into her, through her, liquid heaven so intense it felt as if it came from every part of her body. She had to be melting right then and there, the inferno of their combined passion so hot it felt as if it liquefied her bones, seared her heart, and sizzled her flesh.

The cocks inside her pounded hard and then held, held and pushed, and she could feel the pulsing of their ejaculations, the heat of their seed warming her inside despite the layers of protection between them.

Every tiny speck of strength left her, and she wondered if she would be able to see or hear again. The flash of colors slowly ebbing behind her closed eyelids filled her vision, and the thunder of heartbeats racing in the aftermath of the cataclysm filled her ears.

"Damn it, Susan. Did I hurt you?"

She couldn't move a muscle, but she found in that instant that she could smile. Colt was a strong man. Good to know she could make him lose control.

Still, she didn't want him angry, either with himself or her. "Good." Only one word, she thought it sufficient.

Even as wrecked as she knew he must be, he kept his weight off her. He kissed her shoulder. "It hurt good? Or you're done with me for good?"

She heard the smile in his voice. "Whatever."

Beneath her, Ryder chuckled. "Woman, you're going to kill us all."

"Me?" She inhaled deeply, breathed in the scent of their combined sexual exertions. The aroma immediately tweaked her libido. *If I could bottle that, I'd make a fortune.* "I'm going to kill us? Hey, I'm the only one here who's *not* a professional driller." Both men snorted at that. She thought for a moment, then added, "But the good news is, I don't think your bits are in any danger of breaking from the workout."

They laughed so hard Susan had a bit of a rough ride. Finally, Colt eased himself off and out of her. She heard him head into the bathroom. Ryder lifted her and slid out from underneath her and also headed for the bathroom. Yawning, Susan snagged a pillow, got under the blankets, and rolled over onto her back.

A couple of minutes later, the men crawled into bed beside her.

"I want to head back over to the hospital later," Colt said.

"Nancy is flying in, her plane lands about eight," Ryder said. "She thought if she could be here for Mike, we'd be freed up to do whatever we have to do at the site."

"Yeah, that's good," Colt said.

"We can order in something to eat," Susan suggested. "That would give us time to rest, and then to get in touch with Matthew."

"Your brother booked in here, too?" Colt's question came around a yawn, which in turn made her and Ryder both yawn.

"Likely, since Kelsey made our reservation, she probably got a room for Matt, too. Why?"

"Just thought a face-to-face talk about what they've found so far would be a good idea."

"So would asking for a wake-up call," Ryder said. He turned onto his side and propped his head up on his left hand. The right one he splayed on Susan, his fingers spread wide as they rested on her belly.

"You want to start trying to figure out who has it in for us," Ryder said. "I've been thinking, and I keep drawing a blank."

"Me, too. Just means we aren't asking ourselves the right questions."

"Maybe you two weren't the target," Susan said. Maybe she was being a bit naïve, but she really didn't want to believe that someone meant to hurt or kill either of her men.

"I can't see that anyone would want to hurt Murph," Colt said. "He's the best man I know, period."

"I agree completely," Ryder said. "Not that Colt and I have made a habit of pissing people off. But we're in business, and sometimes, egos intrude."

Susan shivered, a natural response to the specter of danger that had just gotten into bed with them.

Colt mistook her reaction. "You don't have to worry, sweetheart. We won't let anyone touch you."

"Don't you worry about me, wildcatter. Just don't let anyone touch the two of you."

"Trust us. We're not about to let anything happen to us, either. Not now." Ryder's words didn't immediately make sense.

"Not when we've finally found you," Colt explained.

Her men might think they knew what was what, and while she trusted them completely, she figured it couldn't hurt to ask Matthew what he thought about the explosion and the threat to Colt and Ryder.

Of course, they, in turn, seemed hell-bent to make sure that she was kept safe, no matter what. It wasn't that she didn't appreciate that, because she did. In her book, real men took care of their women. She'd grown up with that concept of relationships and responsibility, and she embraced it fully.

But now that she was in love, Susan had discovered another aspect of the male-female dynamic. She was just as determined to do the same for them.

## Chapter 12

Morton Barnes sat on the edge of his chair with a glass of Jack in his hand, absorbing every word of the televised early-evening newscast. The on-air report, live on location from San Angelo to this Houston station, even featured a picture of the man injured in the drilling site explosion.

Until that instant, until disappointment flooded him, Morton hadn't realized that what he really wanted to do was kill either Evans or Magee, or maybe even both of them.

He remembered Michael Murphy, of course. He'd been a what? Retired cop or something. No, Morton mentally amended, actually, Murphy had been an ineffectual tagalong, who, for some reason, those two no-accounts had liked. He'd never paid much attention to the man, possibly because Murphy had made no bones about not liking him. Well, the feeling had been entirely mutual.

Morton wondered if Murphy had been injured badly enough to die, and if he did die, would that hurt his former partners? That would be something, wouldn't it? One strike, one measure of payback. The beginning of the end. The notion pleased him. Yep, maybe if old Murphy gave up the ghost, Evans and Magee would suffer.

*Don't see why they would. The man's just an employee, not anyone important. Not family. So much for your grand plan, Morton. Can't even plant a charge properly anymore, can you?*

"It's not my fault. That stupid secretary said Evans and Magee were scheduled to be at the San Angelo site." Morton shook his head. He wished his father would stop talking to him. It was hard enough to focus on the task at hand without the old man chiming in with his negativity and snide comments every damn minute. He blinked because the newscast had ended, and he realized he might have missed something important. There might be more on the eleven o'clock report. He'd have to be sure to watch it, just in case.

"Hurt their damn bank accounts, no doubt. Debris all over the damn place, that's going to cost some to clean up." No matter what his father said, that was something, a first strike.

In the meantime, he had to think about his next step. Those two bastards hadn't been in San Angelo this morning, but they sure as hell were there now, he'd bet money on it. They'd likely have to hang around for the next couple of days. The authorities would want to question them. Morton rubbed his hands together. He'd done a good job planting those explosives. Maybe *Dos Hombres* would be fined for safety violations. Who's to say that damn place didn't go up because of carelessness on their part? What he'd seen on TV, his bomb had made such a mess, they'd never be able to figure out what happened.

A new thought occurred to Morton, and he stopped and pondered. *Did* he want to kill those bastards right away, or did he want to inflict as much damage as possible, first?

*You need to stop waffling about. You need a plan. How many times have I told you? A smart man not only has a goal, but a step-by-step* plan *to make that goal reality. That's the problem with you, Morton. You couldn't plan your way out of a wet paper bag. Never could, never will.*

"Shut up! I'm not a kid anymore. I've run two successful companies, and all without your fucking help. And what did you ever do, anyway? You inherited all your money, same as me. So you just leave me be, do you hear me, Daddy? You just fucking leave me be!"

Morton blinked. He expected his father to yell right back at him, maybe cuff him a good one because he'd been disrespectful, but for once, the old bastard stayed silent. Morton reached up and rubbed his right temple. His head hurt. He needed some aspirin.

Morton got to his feet, walked to the downstairs bathroom. He reached for the bottle then saw another one, this one a prescription the doctor had given him a few months back when he'd sprained his ankle. Bypassing the aspirin, he took two of the stronger painkillers instead.

He closed the door to the medicine cabinet and caught sight of his reflection. He looked old, old and haggard. He looked…holy hell, he looked like his father. How did that happen? When did that happen?

Morton turned away from the mirror. He'd been going to do something. What was it? Ah, yes, now he remembered. He was going to sit down and detail a plan—a payback plan aimed at the men who'd ruined his life. He was finally going to teach Colt Evans and Ryder Magee a lesson that had been a long time coming, a lesson they wouldn't soon forget.

He still had some explosives left over from when his construction company folded. He was supposed to have seen them all disposed of at the time but, with one thing and another, hadn't gotten around to it. Maybe he'd known he'd have another use for them. Maybe it was fate that he'd held on to them.

He liked the way explosives made his point for him. His thoughts wandered back to the newscast. Yes, he'd have to watch it again at eleven. He'd liked seeing the chaos he had created. He liked knowing his enemies would be running around, trying to figure out what was happening, trying to figure out who was gunning for them.

All those explosives and all the years he'd spent studying construction and how to build things up were going to pay off now, as he tore everything *Dos Hombres* stood for, down.

All he had to do was decide on the best place to strike next.

\* \* \* \*

Colt headed down the hall to the ICU. Mike could only have two visitors at a time while he was in the unit. Given the choice of having the nurse send Nancy out of his room or just one of them popping in, Colt and Ryder decided they'd take turns.

Last night, when they'd peeked in at him, the man had looked like death warmed-over. Seeing him like that had scared them both. The news that Murph had regained consciousness, even if he was still in the ICU, had bolstered them both.

Colt nodded to the charge nurse and then walked to room four. Bracing himself for what he might see, he stepped through the door.

Mike was lying, leg up in a sling, his head turned away from the door as he listened to something Nancy Miller was saying. Something about the way the woman looked at Murph shocked Colt. It would seem the lady had a soft spot for the old man.

"Well, I expected to see a man who's seriously injured. You wallowing in that bed, there, Mr. Murphy?"

"If I was gonna wallow, I'd pick a damn sight more comfortable bed, you can be sure of that, boy."

Colt grinned, for the words were an echo of the past, of the years after two fourteen-year-old street kids had been moved into Murphy's two bedroom house on the edge of El Paso. For the first time in many long years, he and Ryder had a roof over their heads, clean beds to sleep in, and regular meals to fill their bellies.

In return, Murphy had demanded that they toe the line, making them do things like keeping their room tidy, even going to school, for pity's sake. In a heartbeat of time, a dozen pictures of Murphy over the years flashed through Colt's mind. He had said more than once that meeting up with Ryder when they'd been eleven had saved his life. Meeting up with Murphy when they'd been fourteen had *changed* his life. And maybe he'd even saved it, too, because he and Ry had started running down the wrong path when they'd run into Murphy.

He focused back on the man in the bed, looking better this morning than yesterday, but still seeming impossibly old.

"I hear they're going to spring you from ICU later today," Colt forced a cheerful tone, "give you your own private room with a view.

We'll see what we can do about making that bed more comfy for you then."

"Don't need no coddling. Just need to go home. Like my own bed just fine." Mike's expression looked as belligerent as he knew his had looked in the past. *What a strange feeling, that after all these years we might be reversing roles.*

"You listen up, Michael Murphy. You'll be staying in this hospital for however long the doctors say, and that's that." Nancy Miller even wagged her finger as she said that.

Colt raised both eyebrows at Nancy's stringent tone. Murph's face split into a grin. Then he turned to look at Colt.

"She's a feisty little thing, isn't she? Do you know she wouldn't let those investigators in to talk with me earlier? She told them they could damn well wait until I'd been moved out of ICU, and those were her exact words. Should have seen the look on their faces, Colt. Reminded me of when my Momma would put her foot down, right on top of my Dad's."

"Ooh, I am not your mother, Michael Murphy, neither am I about to sit around here being talked about as if I was a piece of furniture! I'm going to get some fresh air. There is way too much testosterone in this room for me right now!"

Of course, as far as Colt was concerned, Nancy then ruined a perfectly good exit line by taking a moment to brush an unruly lock of hair off Murph's face.

Murphy stared at the door where she had exited for a long moment. "Hell of a woman. Never realized—" Murph stopped talking as an expression of embarrassment came over him.

"Sometimes, you just need the right moment to find what's right there in front of you." The idea that there might be a romance brewing between the almost sixty-year-old Murphy and their executive assistant, a forty-year-old widow, thoroughly tickled Colt.

Just thinking of what he and Ryder had found with Susan, he really hoped things went that way for Murph and Nancy. They each deserved to be happy in life.

To save Murph's growing blush, Colt decided to change the subject and tackle what had been on his mind since the day before when he'd first heard about the explosion.

"What the hell happened out there, Mike?"

"Damned if I know." Murphy took a moment to adjust himself in the bed.

Colt had to stifle his urge to help. Murph winced, so movement did hurt, but the man sighed when he obviously found the right position.

"I showed up at the rig right at seven a.m." He continued with his report. "Did the walk around, you know, before the other men arrived—same as we always do. Then I headed into the trailer, thinking to put on a pot of coffee. Next thing I know, I'm lying on the ground outside, halfway to the rig, with pieces of the trailer burning all around me."

Colt shuddered as he envisioned the scene. He recalled the glimpse he'd had of the trailer in the aftermath of the explosion when they'd stopped at the site the day before. There'd been very little left of the metal building. Dr. Scott hadn't been kidding when he said Mike Murphy was a very lucky man.

Colt chose his words carefully. He knew enough about investigations to understand he shouldn't give away too much, not to Mike, not before he spoke to the investigators. "So nothing looked out of the ordinary to you at all?"

"Not one damn thing, Colt. I've been running it through my head, trying to see if I can recall anything unusual, anything suspicious. Trying to figure it all out. But you know me. If I'd thought anything had been off, I'd have taken precautions. I know I didn't smell any gas or anything. Seemed to me the damn trailer went up shortly after I turned on that coffeemaker. If there'd been a gas leak, though, the alarm should have been ringing. Besides, I'd have smelled *something*."

"It wasn't a gas leak, but that's all I know for certain at the moment. Likely, once you get moved, those investigators will be on you like peanut butter on jelly."

"I'll tell them everything I know, of course, but that sure as hell isn't much."

"It'll be enough," Colt assured him. "So how are you feeling? Really?"

Mike made a point of looking toward the door, likely to make sure Nancy wasn't close by or on the verge of returning. "I feel like hell. Like I was rode hard and put away wet."

"You need or want anything, you tell Nancy, she'll see you get it."

"You don't need to go fussing over me," Mike grumbled.

This time, Colt saw the embarrassment and didn't care. He leaned forward. "You listen to me, old man. You belong to me. To me and Ryder. And if we want to fuss over you, we fucking well will, so just deal with it." The wave of emotion swamped him, taking him by surprise. "Jesus Christ, Mike. We could have lost you. God damn it all to hell, we could have lost you."

"Hey. No cussing. There're ladies in the next room. And don't you go getting all teary-eyed, either, boy. I'm not planning on leaving this earth anytime soon. Besides, I have to wait till you boys get yourselves hitched. I figure I'm due being able to bounce some grandbabies on my knee."

It was the closest Mike had ever come to saying out loud that they were a family. Michael Murphy had never once voiced what could only be called the more tender sentiments. He'd never once told them he loved them, but he'd *loved* them every day since the day he'd caught them trying to steal food and brought them to his home.

Colt swallowed to get his emotions under control. Then he said, "Yeah, well, as it happens, Ryder and I have met someone."

Murph never even blinked at Colt's announcement that they had met some*one*. It just proved to Colt—as if he'd needed any—that the man who'd taken them in and become their father, in every way that mattered, knew his sons.

"Is that a fact? Maybe I ought to give this woman a talking to, let her in on a few secrets on how to handle the two of you."

"I've got news for you, old man. She seems able to handle the two of us just fine."

Mike laughed, then groaned with the twinge of pain the laughter caused him. He looked down at his leg, encased in bandages and suspended in a sling. He shook his head, but didn't say anything. He didn't have to. Colt knew the man was pissed at the inconvenience of having a busted leg, more than anything else.

"They get me into a regular room, the two of you bring her on by. I want to meet the woman that can take on the two of you. She sounds like she'd be a woman worth knowing."

Colt laughed. "We'll do that."

# Chapter 13

It looked like a war zone.

What had once been a trailer had been reduced to a piece of jagged metal, lewdly opened as if an oversize can opener had torn into it. Debris littered the ground, and Susan shivered, imagining what it must have been like to be in the midst of it all.

In the middle of the field the derrick stood, dark, tall and eerily idle.

Susan insisted on accompanying the men to the drill site. When they both looked as if they might start spouting "reasons" for her to stay behind at the hotel, she pointed out that, with them at her side and all the investigators on the scene, the drill site was likely the safest place in all of San Angelo for her to be.

When they'd arrived the day before, they'd only stopped off there long enough to find out where their friend, Murphy, had been taken. She'd only gotten a quick glimpse of the devastation. Of course, they'd tuned in to the television news last night, as well. So Susan thought she understood what they'd be seeing in the light of day.

She'd been wrong. Now that she'd listened to some of the stories about Mike Murphy, and about Colt and Ryder's growing up years, the horror of what had happened yesterday morning was that much more real to her.

The entire site had been roped off with yellow police tape. Little markers numbered each piece of debris, still resting on the ground where the blast had strewn them.

A larger marker noted the spot where Mr. Murphy had lain, unconscious. There, the ground had a darker stain, which Susan surmised was blood. Looking down at that stain, Colt went stonily silent while Ryder cursed low and long, finishing with a very ragged, "Jesus Christ, Colt."

"Yeah, I know. Fucking miracle he's alive, let alone not seriously hurt."

As she'd done in the hospital the day before, Susan stood between them, a hand on each of their backs, soothing them in the only way she could in public.

They didn't take long to settle. Susan could almost feel the change of emotion in them, could sense the rage that began to grow in place of the horror and the fear.

"Someone did this to us, to him. They're going to pay." Colt's words held the fervency of a vow.

"Damn straight," Ryder agreed.

As one, her men looked up, looked around, and Susan felt sorry for whichever investigator the two of them cornered. They wanted answers, and they wanted them *now*.

It wasn't investigators their gazes found, however. There, not fifty feet away from them, standing just off to the side and apparently having a conference between them, stood three of Susan's four brothers.

She registered the exact instant that Josh and Alex saw her with Colt and Ryder. The shock that briefly flashed in their eyes confirmed something she'd suspected from the moment she finally remembered those hazy hours after her other brothers' wedding reception.

As natural as breathing, Colt and Ryder took one of her hands each. She kept the smirk off her face when her younger brothers' eyes widened at the sight. Matthew, who had no idea there was any subtext happening around him, nodded as they approached.

"Colt, Ryder. How's your friend doing?" he asked.

"Better, thanks," Colt said. "They'll be moving him out of Intensive Care this afternoon. He'll be off his feet for a few weeks, but he's going to make a full recovery."

"That's good news. I was just going to update Josh and Alex on what the investigators have shared with me so far." Matthew stepped back, making the circle they all stood in larger.

"Susie, what are you doing here?" Alex's gaze went from one of her hands to the other. She could tell he was really surprised to see her there.

"I was just going to ask you and Josh the same thing. Don't you two have an oil company to run? Deals to broker? Lives to orchestrate and direct, like some kind of deity from on high?"

No one said anything for a long moment. Matthew's gaze tracked from Susan to her men. He furrowed his brow, then turned to look at his younger brothers.

"Okay, what did you two clowns do this time?" he asked.

"Do?" Josh looked at Matthew with as innocent an expression as Susan had ever seen him wear. She wasn't fooled, of course, and from the expression on Matthew's face, he wasn't fooled, either.

"What makes you think we did anything?" Alex asked.

"A lifetime of being your older brother," Matthew said.

"I was just surprised to see Susan here, is all," Alex said. "I mean, I know how anxious she was to get that ranch up and running…and all." His voice petered out, and then he cleared his throat.

Matthew put his hands on his hips as he studied the pair.

Susan kept silent. She'd played a version of this game off and on for most her life. Josh and Alex liked to think they were the "fixers" of the family. Most of the time, their idea of what needed to be fixed wasn't necessarily shared by anyone else.

Matthew turned to look at her. "Suse? Care to enlighten me?"

How much did she dare reveal? Part of this story certainly didn't portray her in a very good light. Then she shrugged. What would be the point? "Not particularly."

"Darlin'? Is something going on Colt and I should be aware of?" Ryder's velvet-over-steel voice caused shivers all over her body. She wondered if he could just talk her to an orgasm. Maybe on the phone? She'd have to test the theory.

While she wasn't necessarily all that interested in satisfying Matthew's curiosity, neither would she deny either of her men an answer when they wanted one. "It all turned out perfectly between the three of us. But I guess you should know that my brothers sent you to me believing that if they gave me what I *thought* I wanted, I would realize the error of my ways and want it no more."

"I think you're going to have to explain that in detail later, when we're alone," Colt said. He gave her brothers a good hard look as he said that, and Susan was gratified to see neither Josh nor Alex could look him in the eye. She also agreed with his sentiment. Some things, after all, should remain private.

Matthew closed his eyes and groaned, obviously getting it. "The two of you better get a clue, or you're *never* going to find a woman willing to take you on. Or, if you do find her, you'll have one hell of a time keeping her."

Josh and Alex proved themselves at least marginally trainable, in Susan's opinion, when they had the good sense to look sheepish and say nothing in their own defense.

Susan decided to bring the conversation back on track. "What have the investigators learned so far, Matthew?"

Matthew *tsked*, shaking his head at his brothers, and then turned his attention back to Susan and the wildcatters. "They finished combing the site, and as you can see, they've marked and numbered each piece of debris. They're working on a computer simulation of the blast, based on the location of these pieces, so they can come up, definitively, with an analysis of the type of explosive used, and how much was involved. They don't have everything yet, but they do have a few things. And one of the things they did find was a blasting cap."

"It didn't get destroyed in the explosion?" Ryder asked.

Matthew shook his head. "No, this was an *extra* blasting cap. Asshole must have dropped it when he left the site after rigging the bomb to go off in the trailer."

"So not only an asshole, but a sloppy one," Colt said.

"Why is that important?" Susan didn't understand why her men seemed pleased with this development.

"Because," Matthew answered, "all blasting caps have serial numbers and are registered with the federal government."

"But that means they'll be able to find him. The person who did this!"

"Well, it's a giant step in the right direction," Colt agreed.

"The caps and explosives have likely been stolen," Matthew said, "which is almost always the case. But it will give the authorities a place to start."

When Matthew looked as if he was trying to hold back a chuckle, Ryder said, "What?"

"I overheard some of the forensic guys trying to get into our bomber's head the way they do. Near as they can tell, he did wire the explosives to go off about five minutes after the trailer door was opened. But they couldn't figure the logic of the bomb placement. Me, I just figured the sloppy asshole was also a total fuckup."

"Where'd he place the bomb?" Colt asked.

"On the outside of the water reservoir," Matthew said.

Susan didn't mind admitting she didn't get it. "I suppose that would be a bad choice, in that the water might put out the fire?" she asked.

Ryder laughed. "Or a bad choice if you thought the water reservoir was the propane tank."

Matthew nodded. "That's the scenario I'm going with."

One of the investigators, wearing a blue windbreaker, spotted Colt and Ryder, and began to make his way toward them.

"Gentlemen," the officer handed his credentials to Colt, "I'm Detective Shipton, San Angelo PD. A few moments of your time, please?"

Colt and Ryder each in turn stroked a hand down her back, a kind of nonverbal "we'll-be-right-back".

"I'll be right here." She watched them accompany Detective Shipton over to where a police van had been parked, obviously the place the investigators were using as a mobile base.

"I wonder how soon it will be before they can find the person who did this?" she asked no one in particular.

Matthew sighed. "Not as fast as they show you on television dramas, unfortunately. It could take a while. I'm afraid there's an even bigger question than that, though. And it's a question no one but the bomber can answer."

She didn't need to have that question spelled out for her because she'd been wondering the same thing herself.

Had this attack been a onetime strike, a random act of violence, or would there be another one?

\* \* \* \*

The authorities had questioned Colt and Ryder, both together and separately, for more than an hour. When they were done, both men looked tight-lipped, pissed off, and very weary.

Susan knew just how to fix that. They hadn't bothered to rent a vehicle in San Angelo. Susan didn't often flaunt her wealth. It wasn't a resource she tended to use to accommodate personal whims beyond procuring the necessities of life. She found that to provide comfort and privacy for those she loved, however, she had no qualms whatsoever in pulling out the big guns. While she'd waited for Colt and Ryder to come back to her, she'd arranged to hire a car and driver for the duration of their stay.

It told her how emotionally exhausted her men were that they didn't even comment on the limousine whisking them toward the hotel.

She let them have most of the thirty-minute ride to brood.

"So did they finally eliminate you both as suspects?" she finally asked.

Colt stirred first, shooting her a narrow-eyed stare. "How did you know they considered us suspects?"

"Matthew said that the most usual perpetrators of property damage of this magnitude were the property owners themselves."

"Huh." Ryder straightened up, seemed to come back to full strength before her very eyes. "Never even occurred to either one of us we'd be considered suspects," he said.

"Pissed me off," Colt bit out.

Susan gave him a slow, steady stare. "Gee, I never would have known that, wildcatter."

Colt looked around, seemed to take note of his surroundings for the first time. His only response was to raise one eyebrow. Then he said, "I had wanted to go back to the hospital, check on Mike."

"I called a few minutes ago." Susan could see neither of them was used to being the recipient of some TLC. She guessed they'd have to get used to it. "They're due to move him to a private room in an hour. He's fine, no new problems, just a bureaucratic snafu freeing up a bed for him. I left the message that you'd be by after dinner. Nancy is still with him. She sounds nice."

Ryder nodded. "She is. And sweet on Mike, apparently. I didn't know that."

"That was a surprise for Mike, too," Colt said. Then he smiled, and Susan knew he was going to be all right. "It didn't seem to bother him, especially."

"Some men seem to like having a woman fuss over them," Susan said.

"You about to fuss over us, Ms. Benedict?" Ryder asked.

"Could be," she admitted. "Guess you'll have to just wait and see, won't you?"

She sat between them and stared straight ahead, but she couldn't stop the slow smile from sliding onto her face, neither could she stop from sensing them trading a long, considering look.

"Guess we will," Colt answered for the both of them.

In just a few more minutes, the car pulled up to the hotel entrance. Susan informed the driver they'd be ready to head out again in a couple of hours. She figured that was plenty of time for medicinal sex, followed by dinner.

She'd called ahead, of course, and been meticulous in her instructions. Waiting out in the hot San Angelo sun, she'd had to do something to get her mind off the fact that while she could relax in relative comfort with a cold drink and her brothers close by, her men were being interrogated and, because she did know them, getting mad as hell about it.

They'd done little more that morning than indulge in a quick shower, but they'd all taken note of the large, lovely hot tub installed in their suite.

Colt and Ryder followed her into the bedroom. She felt their eyes on her as she made a beeline to the bedside table, removed the things they would shortly need. She said not a word to them, just headed into the adjoining bathroom. She watched out the corner of her eye as they took note of the candles, the softly playing, smoky jazz, and the wine bucket close to the tub.

She set the supplies on the ledge between the tub and the wall. Then she turned and began, very slowly, to peel out of her clothing.

"A modern day siren, come to lure us into the waves?" Colt asked.

Susan felt her laughter emerge, soft and seductive—because that's how she felt. "But not to your doom," she said.

Oh, their eyes were all on her now as she dropped her clothing on the floor beside her. When she'd skimmed out of her thong and stood naked before them, she allowed her gaze a quick trip down their bodies. Their cocks, hard, pressed against the denim of their pants.

"You can watch me bathe myself. Or you could undress and join me. Your choice."

"Hell of a choice," Ryder said. He looked at Colt. Colt nodded. Together, they began to undress.

"That puts a fantasy in my head," Colt admitted. "Watching you run your hands all over your luscious body, pleasuring us all. We'll save that one for when we get back home."

Did he realize he'd just referred to her ranch as home? Susan doubted it, and she sure wasn't going to press it. She had other things on her mind just then.

If they'd asked her, right at that moment, she would have been unable to lie to them. She'd have to tell them the truth.

Susan Benedict already knew that her home was no longer the ranch she loved on a corner of Benedict land.

Her home was with the men she loved, wherever they wanted to go.

## Chapter 14

*My God, she's magnificent.*

Ryder felt his cock hardening, and as his gaze raked Susan's gorgeous, naked body, he began to imagine the untold delights he would find in her. It didn't take a genius to figure out what she'd done, either. She'd known how aggravating this afternoon had been for him and Colt, and she'd decided she was going to make them feel better.

She'd decided she would take care of them. He found he really liked the feeling.

"Medicinal sex," he said. "I'll take it."

He didn't wait a moment more. He stepped up to her and lifted her into his arms then lowered her gently into the bubbling froth. He stepped in after her and gently eased her onto his lap.

Colt got in and moved to the other side of the tub. "I'm in the mood to watch the two of you," he said. "Don't know why that turns me on so much, but there you have it."

"It's because we're all connected." Susan reached out, reached down, and fisted Ryder's cock. "I guess you could say that when my mom sat me down to tell me the facts of life, she had a bit more to say than most mothers."

Susan looked like she wanted to say more but was holding back. "What else did your momma have to say?" Ryder asked her.

He didn't think the pink on her cheeks was only from the heat of the tub.

"That when it's the right three people, there's an almost spiritual connection, and jealousy doesn't exist. Just the opposite, in fact. That with the right three people, everything they do together is erotic for everyone."

"Makes sense," Ryder said. "Because as much as Colt gets turned on watching you and me, I get turned on watching the two of you."

"Let's give him something to watch, then," she said. She began to stroke him with a slow, sultry caress, her touch stoking the fire of his passion. She knew how to handle him now, how to give him the most pleasure.

He eased her back against him, altering her position just enough that he could open her, both to his touch and Colt's gaze.

He used his right hand to cup her breast, his forefinger and thumb pinching her nipple then pulling it, elongating it. Her breath hitched as he knew it would because he'd already learned she liked this. His left hand began to stroke back and forth across the opening of her slit.

"So, when I buy that paddle, I'm thinking of getting you a set of nipple clamps. Ever worn them?"

"No." Her word came out a breathless sigh.

"Mm, that sounded promising," Colt said. "Do you think you'd like them?"

"Yes."

"Let's see how your pussy feels," Ryder said, close to her ear, and then used his tongue to moisten the shell of it. Susan shivered, and her nipples hardened. "Kiss me, woman."

Instantly obedient, Susan turned her head so that their mouths nearly touched, then stretched her neck to make the connection. He used his tongue to tease and taste and then inserted two fingers into her pussy.

She groaned and arched her hips as his fingers sank deep. Her cunt was so incredibly hot and tight and wet. Feeling her sent his arousal higher. Needing to pleasure her more than he needed to come himself, he began to finger-fuck her, bringing his thumb into play to stroke the hooded nub of her clit.

Ryder gently broke their kiss, his own breath hitching when Susan's hand lost its rhythm on his cock. *She's so horny she can't focus.* He wanted her completely unfocused.

"How many times can the two of us make you come, I wonder?" He said the words close to her ear, smiling when she shivered again.

"The plan was for me...*Oh, God*, for me to pleasure the two of you."

"What makes you think you're not? It's the hottest turn-on in the world to make you come, to watch you come." Colt moved slightly, and Ryder knew his friend likely was as hot as he was.

"Come for us, Susie," Ryder said against her ear. "Come now."

Her hand stilled completely around his cock as she gasped out her orgasm. She closed her eyes and relaxed on him, her head drifting back to find that special cradle against his shoulder. In his arms, she shivered. Around his fingers, her pussy clenched. His reward was a wave of warm, wet nectar, a sweet coating he intended to taste. Her body flushed as she continued to come, and a look of total bliss blossomed on her face.

It made him feel ten feet tall, knowing he could give her the gift of rapture. It also made him harder and hotter than hell.

A quick glance at Colt told him his best friend was experiencing the same reaction.

Susan inhaled deeply as her climax ebbed. Ryder smiled and waited until her eyes fluttered open. Then he slipped his fingers out of her and into his mouth. Her eyes flared, and she licked her lips.

"Sweet," he said to her.

"Now, it's my turn, wildcatter." She slid off his lap into the tub and, in the next instant, took his cock into her mouth.

* * * *

Her body still hummed with the force of her orgasm, her hunger for these men and what they made her feel, not sated, not even by half.

She took Ryder's cock into her mouth, enjoying the challenge of taking him deep when most of his magnificent erection stood beneath the churning water.

"God, you do have a great mouth, sweetheart."

"I don't know what makes the prettier picture," Colt said, "watching you come or watching you suck cock."

Susan nearly smiled. She would have told him, if she could, that she loved sucking cock, and never so much as lately. Something about the taste of both these men fed an elemental hunger within her.

"We're gonna stand up, honey. Nice and easy. Don't stop sucking me."

She kept Ryder's cock moving in and out of her mouth as he eased to his feet. She thought he'd like her to stay on her knees, but when she felt Colt move behind her, felt his hands on her hips, she complied with the unspoken order and stood. Of course, she had to bend over to keep Ryder's tasty self in her mouth. Then she sensed Colt moving to the side, and she understood why her men had changed her position.

A slick whisper of sound followed the tear of foil, and when she felt the heat of Colt's body move in behind her, she spread her legs slightly.

He grasped her hips and guided his latex-covered cock to her slit, then sank deep.

The heat of the water had swollen her delicate pussy lips, making the slide of Colt's cock an even tighter and more delectable sensation than usual.

"Let's see if we can all come together," Colt said.

Ryder's hands grasped her head, his fingers clutching her close. "Yeah, simultaneous orgasms. We'll reach heaven together."

Susan nearly lifted her mouth to tell him he really was a poet at heart. But then Colt reached down and began to stroke her clit. Every thought evaporated, and need, hot, blinding need, filled her.

Ryder's hands on her head helped brace her for Colt's thrusts, now coming hard and fast. He pinched her clit, and in response, she began a steady, slow draw on Ryder's cock, taking him deep, sucking him hard. She felt the warning tingles, heard Colt moan, felt his cock begin to pulse inside her.

Using her right hand, she cupped Ryder's balls while her left reached around behind him so her fingers could play up and down his ass, teasing his anus.

"*Jesus!*" The ephitet exploded from him at the same time as his semen, and Susan drank him, swallowing the first mouthful even as her own climax erupted. Colt held himself still and deep in her cunt, his cock pulsing his ejaculation.

In that moment, Susan's pleasure reached a height she'd never believed existed, rapture so intense because it was shared by the two men she loved.

She released Ryder even as she realized the strength had left her knees. If it wasn't for Colt's grip of her, she'd have fallen face-first into the spa.

"Oh, my goodness." Susan felt so weak she giggled. Ryder sank down so that he was sitting once more on the bench in the spa. He reached for her, gathered her in, and had a good grip of her when the shaking started.

Vaguely, she was aware that Colt got out of the tub. The next thing she realized, he'd returned with a warm towel, and Ryder lifted her into his arms.

"Easy, sweetheart. We have you."

"I don't know why I'm sh–shaking."

"Maybe I fucked you into shock," Colt said as he sat down on the chair in the bathroom and began to blot the water from her skin.

Susan laughed. "You just might have."

Ryder got out of the tub and grabbed a towel, making quick work of drying himself. Despite having had two orgasms in short order, Susan had to admit the sight of one naked male in front of her and the sensation of one under her was turning her on.

"Why don't I just order us some steaks from room service?" Ryder asked.

"I'm starving," Susan admitted around a yawn.

"Sounds good, Ry. After we eat, I'd like to go visit Mike. You up for that, sweetheart?" Colt asked.

"You bet. As soon as I get some food into me, I'll probably perk right up. You both might as well know, I've never been known as a dainty eater."

"Damn good thing," Ryder said. "Never could understand why a woman would want to live on lettuce."

"I'm blessed with a good metabolism," Susan said. "But some women have to battle their weight all their lives."

"Don't see why," Colt said. "God made women, and men, all different sizes. Your body is your body."

Susan leaned up and placed a kiss on his lips. "Thank you. It's nice to know if I suddenly gain weight you won't be tossing me over for a skinnier model."

"Nope. I have the feeling, sweetheart, that you're stuck with the both of us."

* * * *

Colt and Ryder just shook their heads when Susan insisted on stopping at the hospital gift shop before they went up to visit Mr. Murphy. She knew that most men would say they weren't the type to want flowers or that flowers were for women. But she also knew that every man she'd ever given flowers to—up until this point, only members of her family—had been delighted with the gift.

They checked in at the nurses' station, first.

"We're here to visit Mike Murphy. How is he doing?" Colt asked.

The woman behind the desk gave him an unsmiling stare. "That information is restricted to members of Mr. Murphy's family."

"I'm Colt Evans, and this is Ryder Magee."

"Oh! His sons. Well, your father is doing very well. His leg is still sore, but he's off morphine, just taking regular painkillers. We expect he'll be in here another few days yet. The doctor has determined the concussion he suffered was a mild one."

"If he needs anything at all—"

"Don't you worry, Mr. Evans. We're taking good care of Mr. Murphy. He's in room four."

The man in the bed didn't look to be injured at all—well, except for his leg being in a sling and suspended mid-air.

"You're looking better," Ryder said.

"Feeling better, too." He leaned forward and lowered his voice. "Nancy went to get me a burger. Didn't much care for the pabulum they fed me for dinner tonight."

Susan grinned because Mike Murphy reminded her a lot of her Uncle Carson.

Colt performed the introductions. Mike Murphy squinted at her.

"Knew a Caleb Benedict. He was a Texas Ranger. Any relation?"

"Yes, sir. He's one of my dads."

"Well, son of a gun. He was a damn good lawman. Worked with him a couple times when I was on the job in El Paso. That was before I got myself wounded and put on early retirement."

"You didn't tell me Mike had been a cop." Susan looked from Colt to Ryder.

"Likely because then we'd have to explain that he caught us attempting to steal some food from a corner grocery," Ryder said.

"They were a couple of the toughest—and most terrified—fourteen-year-olds I'd ever seen," Mike said.

"You knocked our heads together," Colt's voice turned soft, "then took us home with you."

"Fed us a meal of canned spaghetti and chickpeas. Best meal I'd had in a very long time." Ryder's tone matched his best friend's.

Susan had already understood these men loved Mike Murphy. He truly was their father, in every way that mattered. Just then, she thought she fell in love with him, too. He'd taken in two street kids and literally changed their lives.

"Would have adopted the both of you if'n I'd been able to locate your mothers. As it was, I had to fight damn hard to have you put in my care legally."

"You probably saved our lives."

"Nuff of this maudlin emotion," Mike said. "You two turned out okay, and I'm proud of you both. I'm saying that on account of the fact that I know those investigators put you boys through the wringer today."

"Yeah." Colt sat down in one of the guest chairs then pulled Susan down on his lap.

Susan felt her face color, but Mike just smiled. Then he sobered.

"I told them I didn't see anything, which I didn't. I've been going over every step from the time I parked my car in the roped off parking area until I woke up hurting like hell on the ground."

She listened as Colt and Ryder filled him in on what they did know. Mike just shook his head.

"You knew when you saw me earlier that it had been a bomb, didn't you?" he asked Colt. There was enough of the stern taskmaster in that tone to make Susan grin.

"Yes, sir. We did."

"That's the last time you're going to try and protect me from the truth, isn't it?"

"No promises," Colt said.

"Figured." He looked out the window for a long moment. The sun had set, and the lights of the city had come on, but Susan didn't think he was even taking in the view.

"Guess we got to start thinking who'd want to do such a thing. Usually, something like this is done for profit—or revenge. It's bound to be the latter, since it wasn't the two of you who planted the damn thing."

"Yeah, that's what we figure. But we just can't think of anyone we've pissed off lately," Ryder said.

Mike shook his head. "See, that's civilian thinking for you. Any cop will tell you, it doesn't have to have been *lately*. Some folks, especially sociopaths, can wait years to get their revenge."

Susan shivered. She hated to think that someone had turned to violence to get revenge on Colt or Ryder, for whatever reason.

Because, if that was the case, then what had happened yesterday really was only the beginning.

## Chapter 15

"I can't believe you'd want to spend time with us here," Colt said as he pulled his car to the curb of the street. "It's just an old house we turned into an office."

"No, it's not just an office, it's *your* office. *Your* company." Susan got out of the car and gave him a huge smile.

He was getting pretty addicted to her smiles. Hell, he was getting pretty damn addicted to *her*, period.

"I don't get it, either," Ryder said. He got out of the backseat and stood next to her. "Your family business owns that huge, big ass building downtown. All ours owns is this renovated eighteen-nineties folk Victorian in the Old Sixth Ward."

Susan shook her head. "Look, anyone can build an empire when they start with a fortune. That's not impressive. The two of you literally started with nothing but hard work and sheer determination, and look what you've made! Damn right I want to spend time with you here. I'm proud of you both."

No words had ever touched Colt more. If he hadn't already been in love with this woman, he would have fallen right there and then. He could see by the sheen in Ryder's eyes that his friend felt the same. His friend cupped her face in his hands and laid a gentle kiss on her.

Colt walked around the car and did the same. He needed to set the record straight, though. "You said that anyone can take a fortune and build an empire, but, honey, that's not necessarily so. I've met a few men in my time who started out with that proverbial silver spoon and ended up losing it all through bad decisions and sheer stupidity."

"Damn straight. You can be proud of the success you've had, yourself," Ryder said. "Every business you've taken on, you've improved. That's a talent."

Susan wrinkled her nose. "Alex and Josh think I'm flighty."

"Because you don't stick with one thing? That's not your talent, honey," Colt said. He threaded the fingers of his right hand through her left. Ryder had her other hand. Together, they led her toward the building they'd made into their corporate headquarters.

"Your talent is taking ailing companies and analyzing what they need and giving it to them. That's a hell of a talent to have, too," Ryder said.

"My God, we're all sappy about each other, aren't we?" Susan said.

Colt saw they'd embarrassed her. He grinned. "Yeah, we're sure as hell sappy about you."

He took a moment to let his eyes roam over the two-story pale yellow house they'd turned into their headquarters a few years before. Their company had been gaining in success, and they'd both felt they needed a presence in Houston. So they'd picked up this old house and done the work on it themselves. It had served them well, but success continued to be theirs, and the time had come to think about moving on. Colt sighed because he and Ryder had been putting off the decision to move into larger digs.

This had been their first tangible sign of success, and neither of them really wanted to let it go. Maybe they'd keep it, give it some sort of modified purpose.

Ryder held the door, and they let Susan enter first.

Just inside the front door sat a "parlor" with a couple of comfy chairs and one desk. "Usually, Nancy would be here, manning the fort," Colt explained. "We have a small clerical staff, with most of our employees—drillers and roughnecks—working out in the field."

The young woman who sat behind a large desk was in the process of hanging up the phone. She gave them a big smile. "Hey, guys. How's Mike doing?"

"He's doing good. He'll be in the hospital for a few more days. Then you and Nancy get to babysit him." Colt grinned, because the image of Mike being housebound for a few weeks kind of tickled his perverse sense of humor.

"Trina, this is Susan Benedict. Susan, Trina Gonzales, accounting clerk extraordinaire."

"Pleased to meet you." Susan extended her hand.

"Same here." Trina shook her hand then picked up two stacks of message slips, handing one to Colt and the other to Ryder.

"We'll be in back if anyone needs us," he said, "going through our archives. But we're still unavailable to the press." There'd been a couple of messages at the hotel in San Angelo. He and Ryder had decided to keep mum, let any and all comments about the explosion come from the investigators. He led the way to the back of the house, where he and Ryder had their offices.

They'd stayed hands-on enough right from the beginning, so pulling all their old files and going through each job wasn't straying into foreign territory.

"I like the way the two of you share this big space, rather than having separate cubbyholes for personal offices," Susan said. She wandered from his desk to Ryder's, looking at everything.

"In the beginning, we weren't here much. Bought and refurbished this place to have a presence in this city that is so central to the oil industry," Ryder said. "And when we were here, it was to plan our next moves, so it made sense to share space."

He came over to the file cabinets and looked at them. "Where do we start?" Ryder asked him.

"I guess at the beginning."

"The first beginning or the second beginning? Because if it's the first, the only ones who got pissed off with us were us," Ryder said.

Colt laughed and counted it a sign of his maturity that he *could* laugh. "True. So I guess we start at the second beginning."

"You know you're going to have to explain that," Susan said.

"We actually started out, more than a decade ago, as *Tres Hombres*," Colt said as he grabbed a big handful of files, then moved aside as Ryder did the same. "There were the two of us, of course—we'd learned the business as roughnecks, working long hours in crappy conditions for outfits that didn't pay a whole hell of a lot. And we had a partner."

"Partner." Ryder said the word as if it were a smelly substance on the ground not to be stepped in. "Every time I think of that bastard, I feel the urge to puke." Then he looked up and gave Susan a smile. "Speaking of those with silver spoons in their mouths trashing their inheritance with bad decisions and stupidity, I think Morton Barnes is the president of the club."

"Should I have heard of this scion?" Susan asked.

"As it turns out, he only finished the job his daddy started of decimating the family fortune. We didn't know that at the time, though. He came to us, offering to help finance us. We struck a deal, all legal and everything."

"So what happened?" Susan asked.

"Asshole was looking for instant returns. He bailed on us, just before our first well came in. We had to pull out of the job—lost that derrick, too, the first big one we ever got. Client hired a bunch of roughnecks, they brought the well in a week later."

"He shouldn't have been able to do that—just bail on you that way," Susan said.

Colt smiled because he'd bet the lovely Ms. Benedict knew more about contracts and clauses than most. "Truth of the matter is, he cleaned out the account, which was against the terms of the contract. Got his original investment back plus a couple of grand extra. Left us holding the bag on a loan, and we had to go back to being roughnecks on somebody else's payroll for a two and a half years to pay it all off."

"Then we began again," Ryder said. "This time, just the two of us."

"And you never went after Barnes?"

Colt could feel her outrage from across the room. "You have to remember, at the time, we were just a couple of roughnecks from the wrong side of the tracks over in El Paso, and Morton was a Barnes of the Houston Barneses."

"Karma's a bitch, though," Ryder said. "Last I heard, he was damn near bankrupt. His second wife scalped him in the divorce, and his latest venture—a brokerage company—went belly-up."

"Well, good." Then she winced. "I really hate to say that, but I really do believe in the law of sowing and reaping."

"Sometimes that law doesn't work," Colt said. "In this case, it took another eight or so years to catch up with that sniveling little bastard."

"Well, I certainly see what you meant by the only ones being pissed off were the two of you."

"Exactly. So we'll go through every job we did, starting with the second."

"What about employees?" Susan asked. "Maybe someone on the payroll now who's not happy or someone who got let go who's held a grudge?"

Colt shook his head. "Hate to think that someone who worked for us could have done this. But yeah, I guess we've got to look there, too." He set aside the folders he was going to look through, then went to his desk and picked up the phone. He told Trina what he wanted. She told him she'd get it all together and send it as an e-mail attachment.

"So, none of the rest of your records are on disc?" Susan asked.

"Nope. I told you, we're just a couple of wildcatters."

Susan pulled a chair over to Ryder's desk and reached for some files. "In that case, you need all the help you can get," she said.

Colt thought truer words had never been spoken.

\* \* \* \*

Susan exited the office and stood on the veranda in the old neighborhood, taking a moment to appreciate the different examples of architecture. Most of the homes were homes, but a few had been remodeled to house small businesses.

Ryder and Colt came out to join her. "So now what?" she asked.

"Now, I guess, we leave everything in the hands of the investigators," Colt said. "Maybe I'd feel differently if we'd found something that stood out."

"Yeah, that was a nice walk down memory lane," Ryder said, "but nothing stood out for me, either. Let's hope when the cops piece together the clues they got from the scene then add in all that data we just sent them, they'll be able to find something."

"Do you want to head back to San Angelo tonight?" No one in the family was using the jet. It would take a couple hours, but she could have it ready if that's what they wanted to do.

"No, Mike's fine," Colt said. "I spoke to him a few minutes ago. He said he's had a fair number of visitors today already and it's tired him out." Colt's brow furrowed, and Susan had to fight the urge to step up to him, smooth it over.

"He's getting old, damn it," Ryder said then.

"Yeah." Colt obviously wasn't any happier about that fact.

Susan could understand their emotions. There were times when she'd notice her fathers had gotten older, and that realization was humbling.

"Tell you what," Ryder came over and stroked his hand down Susan's back, sending delightful shivers down her spine, "let's spend the night here in town, then we can make our way back to Lusty in the morning."

"Sounds like a plan. We can have our pick of a couple of apartments the family maintains here in Houston," Susan said. Every so often, she found it very convenient that she did have such a vast array of resources to fall back on.

"Well, now, that would be nice. But it just so happens, there's another house."

"Another house?"

"When the business began growing so that staying here overnight became impractical for us, we bought a house for ourselves. To live in," Colt said.

Susan looked from one to the other of them. They'd admitted to being closer than brothers since the time they were each about eleven.

"The two of you have always lived together, haven't you? Even when you got to the point where you could afford to do otherwise."

"We've bunked together since that first big piece of cardboard in the alley behind Guido's restaurant," Colt said.

"Yep, and the minute we began bunking together, our luck changed. No need to disturb a winning pattern."

"I have a feeling the two of you have more than one interesting story to tell," Susan said.

"Could be." Ryder's response was laconic, but the twinkle in his eyes told her he was likely thinking of some of those stories right then.

"Come on, sweetheart." Colt picked up her right hand and kissed it. "It's been a long, boring day. Let's go home and see what we can do to liven things up some."

"All right." Susan turned and stretched up to place a light kiss on his lips. Then she turned and did the same to Ryder. "Let's go home."

Susan found herself wondering during the short drive just what sort of house two thirty-something bachelors would share. Would they go for ultramodern, a condominium where landscaping would be done by others, or would they choose something of a Tuscan flavor in one of the new exclusive developments that had begun to spring up in the last few years?

Neither, she realized a half hour later when Colt wheeled his Buick into the driveway of a very nice middle-class family home. Two-story, brick, with shade trees in front and what appeared to be a fenced backyard, it seemed like the kind of place a body would feel good coming home to each night.

Susan imagined that for the homeless boys still inside the men, this home, more than anything else they'd ever accomplished, had been their dream come true.

"Very nice." She got out of the car and stretched her muscles.

"Just over three thousand square feet, with four bedrooms. It was the first house we looked at," Ryder said. "We just needed a place to call home, to kick back."

"And to have a place for Mike to stay when he came to visit?"

"Yeah." Colt smiled. "Stubborn old coot insists on living in El Paso. That's fine for now, but we both know there'll come a day when he'll need family closer by than that."

"Course, if he insists on staying in El Paso, then we'll deal."

"But since you already have a place for him…" Susan let the sentence fall. It didn't surprise her in the least they'd consider the man who'd taken them in when they bought their first real home.

She reached into the car and pulled out her overnight bag. "I hope you have a washer and a dryer, because I am out of clothes."

"You're not going to need clothes, Ms. Benedict." Ryder slid a hand down her back, brushed it across her ass. Just that quickly, Susan was aroused.

Susan laughed and skipped away from him. "Oh, no, you don't, Mr. Magee. I'm wise to your tricks. If I let you, the two of you will have me flat on my back the minute we get inside the house."

"Your point?" Colt took a step to bring him even with Ryder. Then they both began to come toward her, predatory gleams in their eyes.

"My point is, I want to see your house, first." She turned away from them and headed toward the long, curved walkway that led toward the front door. The men weren't far behind, and she thought briefly about breaking into a run, but they had to unlock the door, anyway. She took the first of three wide steps and stopped when her leg hit some kind of wire.

"Huh. I wonder what—"

"Jesus!" Colt's curse and his tackle hit her at the same instant, and she landed on him on the grass, the wind knocked out of her as he rolled with her away from the house.

The world exploded in a maelstrom of thunder, fire, and brimstone.

## Chapter 16

Morton wanted more than anything to drive past the house on Barclay Drive. He knew those bastards were back in town. Posing as a reporter, he'd called their office and the receptionist had confirmed their arrival but had refused to put his call through. Said they were too busy to talk to the press.

Just as well. He didn't want to speak to them. He just wanted to kill them.

Morton chuckled. "I don't wish to speak to them, my dear. I only want to kill them!" He laughed and laughed until he had tears in his eyes. Finally, he got his mirth under control. He really wanted to go and see firsthand the result of his labors.

Dark had fallen, and they should have been home by now and received his gift. Or maybe he'd get there just in time to watch it happen!

He'd spent the morning rigging the explosive, using some of the last of his C4 and a remote detonator. One of the things he'd loved best about the construction company he'd owned was those times he got to play with the explosives.

He loved the power of them, and he loved his power over them. He felt the need to drive past their house, see how well he'd crafted that surprise for the bastards.

*Don't be a fool. Dumb ass bastard, returning to the scene of the crime. That's what all the low-life criminals do. They return to the scene of the crime, and then they get caught.*

"I'm not a criminal. Those two no-accounts are just getting what they have coming to them, is all. They ruined my life, made me a laughingstock, took me for a ride then used my name to gain entrée into Houston business circles. Now shut up, Daddy, and leave me alone!"

He didn't care what his father said. This was a free country, wasn't it? He was a citizen of this city, of this great state of Texas, of this country, and if he wanted to go for a ride about town in Bessie, well, then, by damn, he could do that, couldn't he?

*At least don't take the damn Caddy. Fucking monstrosity stands out like a sore thumb. Someone might have seen it earlier when you planted the bomb, too.*

"Shows what you know. I'm smarter than you ever gave me credit for. I parked two blocks away from the house, and I wore a pair of green coveralls the gardener left behind. I was just another servant, going about his miserable life. No one ever looks at servants."

By damn, he would take that drive. He deserved to bask in his own glory after all these years.

Morton took a few moments to make sure his appearance, as always, was pristine. His father had hammered into him the importance of personal hygiene and a neat appearance. It didn't matter if he was headed out the door to put gas in the car or to go out to the club for lunch. He was a Barnes of the Houston Barneses and, therefore, expected to set an example.

Morton ensured his suit hung well, that his hair was combed neatly, and his Stetson sat just so upon his head. Nodding his satisfaction, he grabbed his keys off the front entrance hall table.

Once outside, he took a moment, as he often did, to admire his car. He'd bought the 1976 Cadillac Eldorado the day after he came in to the last part of his trust, when he'd been thirty. It had been in mint condition, and he'd paid a pretty penny for it, but that didn't matter one damn bit. It was the only car he'd ever really wanted and the only car that fit his style.

Its white body gleamed with not a mark or dent upon it. He patted the hood and admitted things would have been a lot easier if he'd realized from the beginning that Bessie—named for his dear, departed grandmother who'd left him that lovely trust—was the true love of his life, instead of getting married two times.

Morton got behind the wheel, and a sense of power, of entitlement, swept through him. He never felt so much a man as when he was behind the wheel of his Caddy. Head held high, he wheeled the big car out of his driveway, heading west.

He supposed it *was* possible that he'd be stopped on Barclay Drive. Yes, likely there would be emergency vehicles on the scene, and they would be stopping traffic, maybe even redirecting it. Perhaps he wouldn't actually be able to drive *past* the house, but he'd get to see a bit of the chaos he created. That would have to be good enough until the eleven o'clock news.

Just in case, he angled his rearview mirror so that he could see his own reflection. And as he drove, he practiced looking shocked and dismayed in the face of the human tragedy he hoped he was about to witness.

* * * *

Susan's ears had finally stopped ringing.

She sat on the camp stool Ryder had gotten for her out of the garage with a fire department blanket wrapped around her and watched the controlled chaos taking place on her men's front lawn.

Beside her, on another stool, Colt was being treated by paramedics for cuts and burns he'd suffered when the front door of the house had exploded. He'd been hurt saving her life.

"Ouch, God damn it, take it easy there!"

There was nothing wrong with Colt's voice, or his temper, Susan thought.

"Don't be such a pussy. Hush up and let the nice paramedics treat you," Ryder said.

"Fuck you," Colt replied.

"Sorry, this door don't swing both ways." Ryder flashed a grin at Colt.

"Ha ha."

Susan recognized scared man macho-banter when she heard it. She did, after all, have four brothers and two fathers. She watched the EMT treating Colt. "Should he go to the hospital?" she asked him.

"I'm not going to a fucking hospital," Colt said.

Susan laid a hand on his leg. "I wasn't speaking to you, sweetheart. I was asking the medical professional amongst us."

The EMT obviously found their kibitzing amusing, unable or unwilling to restrain his smile. "Mr. Evans has suffered only superficial injuries, a few small cuts and just a couple of light burns. He's going to hurt like hell for a day or so, and you might want to contact his doctor to get him some pain medication. But I really don't think he needs to go to the hospital."

"I don't need any pain pills, either," Colt said.

Now he sounded more like Benny when the little guy was told to get ready for his bath. Susan caressed Colt's leg. "You might change your mind. Wouldn't hurt to have some on hand, would it?"

A squeal of tires caught Susan's attention. She turned to see that a familiar looking Hummer 3 had pulled up to the curb. Both driver and front passenger doors were flung open, and her brothers Alex and Josh emerged.

They easily evaded the police trying to keep out nosy neighbors. She heard the word "family", which made her smile.

"Holy shit! What the hell happened here?" Alex asked.

"Colt saved my life," Susan said before either Colt or Ryder could take over the conversation. It was very important to her that these brothers, who had seemed a little miffed a couple of days ago, understand just what had really happened here.

Her brothers both focused their attention on Colt.

"To answer your question," Colt said, "what happened here was a goddamned bomb."

"How badly are you hurt?" Josh asked him. Then he looked over at Ryder. "You?"

"No, I was further away and hit the ground the instant I understood what the hell was happening."

Josh moved to stand beside Colt, as if he would watch over him, and Susan wondered whether her men understood they had just gained a whole mess of family.

"Just minor," Colt answered him. "More of a nuisance than an injury, really."

"What about you, little sister?" Alex squatted in front of her.

Susan shivered as those moments when she'd hit the wire and Colt had grabbed her replayed in her memory. She didn't think she'd ever forget the fear and the explosion if she lived to be a hundred. She put her attention back to her brother.

"I'm older than you, remember? I'm not hurt at all, just shaken up."

Susan returned her focus to the house. The fire department and police had arrived within minutes of the blast. There hadn't really been as much of a fire as she would have expected, and it didn't appear as if the explosion had been big enough to damage anyone else's property.

Ryder laid his hand on her shoulder. "You warm enough, sweetheart?"

"I'm okay. I'm not shaking from the cold. I'm shaking from being scared and being mad. I know what this place means to you both, and it pisses me off that someone would do this."

"It does mean a lot to us, but it's just a house, Susie Q. We'll do what has to be done to fix it," Ryder said.

"Fucking asshole's a dead man when I get my hands on him." Colt's tone sounded icier than she'd ever heard it. When she looked over at him, he said, "I don't care about the fucking house. I care about you. You could have been killed, goddamn it."

Susan felt her eyes tear. "But I wasn't. You took care of me."

"Excuse me."

Susan looked up and into the eyes of a large man wearing a black windbreaker with a tie peeking through the zippered opening.

"I'm Detective Carrerra, Houston PD." He flashed his credentials, but Susan noticed no one in particular really looked at them.

"First off, we're going to have to restrict access to the property until our investigation is complete. You'll have to find some other place to stay for the foreseeable future. Now, who'd like to tell me what happened here tonight?"

For all his anger, Colt was able to give a succinct, if terse account. He also reached into the back pocket of his jeans and pulled out his wallet.

"You might want to contact Detective Shipton of the San Angelo PD."

"And why would I want to do that, Mr. Evans?" Carrerra asked as he took the card.

"Because this is the second bomb we've had directed toward us in three days. Call me fanciful, but there might be a connection."

Despite the situation—or maybe because of it—Susan found Colt's dry tone particularly funny. She did her best, however, to suppress the urge to laugh.

Laughing hysterically might get her hauled away for a psychiatric examination. Fortunately, her brother Alex turned to the detective.

"I'd like very much to get my friends and my sister settled for the night, detective. If you need them, they'll be in penthouse three of Benedict Towers."

The detective raised one eyebrow and made a point of looking around the neighborhood. "I'd say that's a quite a move up for you, gentlemen. Congratulations."

Susan blinked twice and then slowly got to her feet. One part of her was glad he'd mouthed off. His attitude had cured her of the need to giggle. She felt conscious of both her brothers moving slightly and even heard Josh's, "Oh, oh."

"Perhaps it would be a better use of your time to question the neighbors, *detective*, as opposed to baiting the victims of this crime. Someone set a bomb on this property, likely today sometime. That means somebody had to have seen something."

"Susie." Ryder's voice reached her through the roiling fury. "It's all right, sweetheart. Let the man do his job."

Susan turned to meet Ryder's gaze. "That would be refreshing." When she met the detective's gaze again, she was gratified to see that he blinked first.

"Mr. Evans is good to go," the EMT said, effectively breaking the tension that had engulfed them.

"Let's go," Josh said. "I'll drive the three of you in the Hummer, and Alex will drive your car." He'd directed his words at Colt, who'd slowly gotten to his feet.

"Yeah. Okay. Thanks." But Colt didn't move, he just looked at Detective Carrerra. "We want to get Susan away from here, if it's all right with you?"

The man nodded, and Susan wondered if it was because he didn't want to listen to any more of her acerbic tongue. She made a mental note to call her father and see if he could do anything about this situation. Having the integrity of her men questioned, even if it was standard police procedure, infuriated the hell out of her.

She felt stiff, likely because she'd been sitting in the cool night air for so long, but turned to walk toward her brother's car.

Ryder and Colt immediately flanked her, with Josh in front and Alex in back. Not that she didn't appreciate the precaution, but likely the coward who'd planted these two bombs was long gone.

Colt got in the front seat of the Hummer. Susan sat in back and watched Ryder jog back to Colt's car. He rummaged in the trunk then came back with a T-shirt that he tossed to his partner.

"Thanks." Colt hissed as he pulled it on, and Susan decided right then and there she was going to insist on pain meds for him.

"I guess there's no doubt that, somehow or other, pal of mine," Ryder said, "we've made it on to somebody's shit list."

"The first thing we have to do," Colt said, "is make sure Susan's safe." He said that to her brother, who nodded enthusiastically. "We have to find someplace to stash her so she's protected. Then we have to do what we can to find out who's behind this. I don't trust the police to give it their all. Especially if Detective Carrerra is involved."

"Susan is right here," she said out loud, "and nobody is stashing me anywhere. That is, of course, unless you two are willing to be stashed with me."

"I'm not hiding," Colt bit out.

"Neither am I," Ryder said.

"Well, that makes three of us. So let's stop talking about what's not going to happen and start trying to figure out who's behind all this."

Colt looked over at Joshua, who had sighed in resignation. "Is your sister always so stubborn?" Colt asked.

Josh flicked a glance at her in the rearview mirror, meeting her gaze. "Yes, unfortunately. But I have to concede her point. Facing trouble head-on is the Benedict way."

Susan smiled. Having won that skirmish, she let Ryder pull her into his arms. "I think we should call the dads," she said. "They might have an idea or two how we should proceed."

"Maybe your fathers will be able to help us convince you to stay out of sight." Colt's low grumble reached her from the front seat.

"Obviously you haven't met my dads." Despite everything, that was something she was looking forward to.

## Chapter 17

It wasn't that Colt didn't appreciate the conference call Josh and Alex set up with Jonathan and Caleb Benedict, their fathers. He did, and Caleb's promise to reach out to some of his contacts and see what could be done to expedite things was a gift Colt didn't think he could ever repay.

But he was anxious to be alone with his family.

*His family.* He'd thought of Ryder that way since before they went to live with Mike Murphy. He and Ryder had found each other at a time when they were both alone, neglected and abused boys. They'd become brothers by choice. Family.

This was the first time he'd extended that definition to include a woman. Of course, Susan Benedict wasn't just any woman. She was *the* woman. Not just the woman who had made his and Ryder's family complete, but the woman they would spend the rest of their lives with.

He still wasn't sure what kind of a husband or father he'd make. Thinking about that made him nervous as hell. What did he know about being a dad? He'd never had one, himself. He guessed there'd be time to worry about that later if, down the road, Susan decided she'd stay with them.

For right now, tonight, he'd been watching Susan ever since she walked to Josh's car a couple of hours before, and he had his suspicions about just how "all right" she really was.

Finally, after the senior Benedicts had been contacted, listened to, and had advised, after a prescription for pain medication had been arranged for and delivered, and pizza brought in and consumed, the younger Benedict brothers left. Clothing and other essentials would be delivered in the morning, but for the night, they'd be fine.

"We should make a list of all the things that need to be done in the morning," Susan said, and to him at least, her smile seemed overly bright. "You'll want to contact your insurance company, although you may get a bit of a hassle because of the criminal investigation. If that happens—"

"Susie?" Ryder's voice sounded quiet, and Colt smiled because that one quality told him Ryder had the same suspicions he did.

"Yes, Ryder?"

"Where exactly does it hurt, babe, and how bad?"

Susan blinked, resembling a wide-eyed owl. Her face went blank, and Colt would bet she was working so hard at trying to be in control of her discomfort she didn't even realize she'd gotten sloppy at her attempts to hide it.

"Um, I'm just a bit stiff, is all. Nothing much."

*Stiff my ass.* In a heartbeat, Colt understood not so much where and how much she hurt, but where and how she'd *gotten* hurt. He would never forget those horrible seconds when he'd looked down, seen that trip wire against her leg. He'd reacted on instinct and with as much speed and agility as possible, but he hadn't been gentle in the process.

"Come here, sweetheart." He didn't get up from his place on the love seat and kept his tone deliberately soft. When she got up stiffly and then walked over to him, he began to undress her. Since Ryder came to stand directly behind her, she couldn't escape. As if realizing the game was up, she sighed and closed her eyes.

The woman was covered in bruises. He'd taken the worst of the impact, both of the explosives and hitting the ground, but he'd rolled them both away from the house, which meant he'd rolled himself on top of her.

He had done this to her, damn it.

"Stop. That's why I didn't tell you, because I knew you'd get that haunted look on your face. You saved my life, Colt Evans. Do you think I give a good damn about a few bruises?"

"*I* give a damn, Susan. I very much give a damn. Come on, now, let's see the rest of it." He and Ryder finished the task of stripping her. Bruises covered both hips and a spot just under her breasts where his arms had banded around her when he'd grabbed her and thrown them both to the ground. She had a scrape on her right knee and one her left elbow, both of which looked raw.

"I'm sorry that I hurt you, sweetheart."

"It really is all right. This is a much better outcome than being blown to smithereens across your front yard."

"*Oh, God.*" Because he could see that so clearly, because she had come close to just such a fate, Colt closed his eyes and shuddered.

Susan stepped closer to him and wrapped her arms around him. "I shouldn't have said that. I'm sorry. I'm sorry."

"I thought I'd lost the both of you." Ryder's voice sounded raw. "I understood in a heartbeat what was happening, and I was too fucking far away to get to either of you."

Colt looked up at his best friend. Ryder's expression underscored the words he'd just said. The two of them were closer than brothers—closer because they'd chosen each other, clung to each other when they'd had nothing else. Now, together, they'd both fallen for the same woman.

They'd all been through hell, one way or another, tonight.

"I think we all got the shit scared out of us," Susan said. She wiped tears from her face, sniffed, and then inhaled deeply. "The important thing is that none of us was seriously hurt. Let's go soak in the spa and then just go to bed. I really need to feel the two of you on either side of me tonight."

"That sounds like a damn good plan," Colt said.

* * * *

They didn't make the tub as hot as they normally would. Susan had gotten a good look at Colt's back. Turnabout was, after all, fair play. The burns were higher up, on his shoulders. But cuts and gouges speckled him.

He hissed a little when he slid into the water. Then he relaxed back and sighed.

Susan situated herself where she liked best to be, in between these two strong men. She'd taken a moment to put some music on the sound system that piped through the apartment—tonight, soulful jazz. Now, she closed her eyes and let the water and the music and, most especially, the company, soothe her.

"I keep asking the same question," Ryder said.

Susan knew he was thinking about the attacks. How could he not be?

"You mean, why us?" Colt asked him.

"No, not that so much. Not 'why us'. You know me. I'm constantly amazed that we survived long enough for Mike to take us in, in the first place. I never did figure we were due more than shit for luck. I'm more surprised when things go well for us than when life craps on us."

Colt chuckled. Susan could only shake her head. "A real pessimist, are you, Mr. Magee?"

"I prefer to think of myself as a realist, Ms. Benedict," Ryder said. "And I'll have you know the one good thing about being a pessimist is that you're never disappointed."

"I suppose I could give you that," she said, "but it's very small comfort."

"So, what question do you keep asking yourself?" Colt asked.

"Why now? What's changed that this is happening *now*?"

Susan opened her mouth and then closed it again. She really didn't think her having entered these men's lives would have prompted anyone to attack them. She had no shadows in her past. The couple of relationships she'd been in had ended amicably enough.

"That is a good question," Colt said. "The only thing that comes to mind is the deal we signed with Benedict Oil and Mining."

Susan turned her head and looked at Colt. He met her gaze.

"There was a huge write-up about it in the *Houston Chronicle*. Benedict Oil is one of the companies to have done well during these last couple of years. And so, by the way, is *Dos Hombres*. That's good business news, and the deal has received a lot of press."

"We'd always operated as if tough times were just around the corner," Ryder said. "So when tough times actually arrived, we were prepared."

He lifted his hand from the water and stroked a dripping finger down her nose. "You might say that was my pessimism at work."

"Do you think that could be it, though?" Susan stretched out her right leg, examined the scrape on her knee, then lowered her leg into the water again. "I mean, I'm not unaware of how tough so many people have had it these last two years. So many people out of work, so many homes foreclosed on. It's heartbreaking, no doubt about it. But why would someone pick on you just because you've been successful?"

"Jealousy, maybe." Colt shrugged then sucked in a breath when that unthinking action obviously hurt. "Seeing our success, could be someone's made us a target out of spite. If that's the case, and it's a random thing…hell, how would we ever find out who it is?"

"I guess our only hope is that whoever it is got sloppy again and left lots of clues," Susan said.

"I hate feeling useless," Colt said. "Waiting around for this asshole to make another move. I'd much rather be doing something about it. Point me in a fucking direction, and let me fix it."

"Damn straight," Ryder said.

Susan could hear and feel the tension seething from her men, which in her mind defeated the entire purpose of soft music and hot bubbling water before bed.

She supposed there was only one thing for her to do. She needed to take the situation in hand, so to speak.

"There's nothing any of us can do tonight." She kept her voice sounding quiet and reasonable. "In the morning, we'll go to Lusty, meet with my dads. We'll contact the investigators and see if there's been any progress. But for now…" She said nothing more, just reached out her hands and captured two not-entirely-soft male cocks.

"You meaning to distract us with sex?" Colt asked.

"Oh, absolutely," Susan said.

"Good," both men said at the same time.

Susan felt her smile stretch wide. "I'm so pleased my little plan meets with your approval, gentlemen." Since she chose that moment to begin to stroke and squeeze, neither man's response came out particularly clear and lucid.

She loved the feel of their cocks in her hands, the way their cocks swelled for her, strengthened for her. The silkiness of the water complemented the silkiness of their male flesh. She thought it a wonder that just here, from where the very definition of masculinity stemmed, that the texture of the male skin could be so soft to the touch.

Closing her eyes, she let her senses guide her, the pulsing of cocks, the hitching of breaths. She could do this, devote her entire attention to pleasuring them, because she loved them. She was only mildly aroused herself. Being a woman, she garnered another kind of sexual pleasure by stroking her men to full arousal. It felt just as primitive, this sense of caring for her lovers as no one else could, of giving them a singular surcease. It fed a wholly feminine need in her as necessary as the need to climax.

For this one night, it would be enough.

Closer now to rapture, her lovers reacted with equal ardor as they began to thrust into her hands. Her thumbs stroked over the tops of their cocks, spreading the viscose lubricant they gave her, inhaling deeply as the scent of them, these men she loved, permeated the moist air around her.

On her downward stroke, she extended a single finger on each hand, using them to caress scrotums that felt hot and full, and her men both groaned in appreciation.

She knew how to touch them now, could easily give each that little extra pressure or elongated caress they craved.

Ryder put his hand over hers, not to stop her but to silently ask for a firmer hold. She gave him what he needed then offered Colt the same.

Wordlessly, they neared their pinnacles, and Susan opened her eyes, gazed at first one and then the other of her lovers. Ryder and Colt wore similar expressions of need, of striving, eyes closed and heads back. Their breathing rasped, just a little, as their chase began.

Faster, firmer, her thumb braiding over equally hot and primed cockheads, she brought them both to climax, savoring the moment when they stiffened, groaned, and granted her the gift of their seed.

"Jesus, woman, you take me apart and put me back together every damn time," Ryder said.

"Damn straight." Colt stole Ryder's usual quip.

Susan felt her smile spreading. Yes, for this one night, it was definitely enough.

* * * *

Damn their fucking lucky hides! Morton knocked back another shot of Jack. He'd managed to drive past the house on Barclay Drive and was left wishing he hadn't. How could that house still be standing? How could those bastards have escaped without so much as a trip to the emergency room?

*You're a complete and total loser. You can't do one damn thing right, can you? All your big talk about your power over the explosives and you don't have one fucking clue what you're doing.*

"Shut up! I planted that C4 right! Must have been something wrong with that batch, or maybe it was the wire. Could happen to anyone."

*And yet it only happens to you.*

"Shut the fuck up! Shut up, do you hear me?" Morton hurled his empty glass against the wall. It crashed against the baseboard, shards of glass and the stench of Jack going everywhere. It had to be this library, he thought. He grabbed the half-full bottle and retreated to his den. He still had a chair there, and his television.

Picking up the remote, he turned it on then selected the news network. He sat down, watching the headlines and the stories while his mind wandered. Those bastards were pissing him off. First, they weren't on the site where they were supposed to be, and now, somehow, they had escaped getting killed at their own house.

What kind of grown men share a house, anyway? Morton shook his head. A picture on the news grabbed his attention, and he focused on the story. Yes, there. That was it!

He listened, perusing the scene—lots of fire trucks there, even an EMT vehicle. The news camera caught the three people huddled in the driveway, a paramedic hovering. He recognized Evans and Magee straight off. He laughed because those two surely didn't look very happy. No, siree, they didn't look happy at all.

Then he noticed the woman with them, caught her in profile as she turned to say something to Evans. Morton realized she was the same woman he'd seen with those two on the news report from San Angelo. She'd seemed familiar to him then somehow, as if he'd seen her or met her at some point.

Putting his attention back on the screen, he had that sense again now. As he watched, Magee put his hand on her back, and she looked up at him and nearly right into the camera.

Recognition hit him. My God, that was the Benedict woman, the daughter of the wealthy family from out Waco way. He'd figured a woman of her background would have better morals than to be going around with a man like Ryder Magee.

He narrowed his eyes, tried to recall the images he'd seen the other day of her. Yes, then it had seemed to him she'd been with Evans.

Didn't matter. Morton perked up when the on-site reporter began to speak.

"...so far, Anthony, there've been no real leads in this attack. Although police refuse to comment on whether or not they're looking for a white Cadillac or Lincoln seen in the vicinity just hours before the blast."

Morton shivered. No! Damn it, he'd been so clever! He got up and turned off the television.

It might be smart to get out of Houston for a little while. Only for a few days until things blew over.

"Until things blow over." He laughed out loud at the joke he'd made. Then he sobered. He knew just where he'd go, too. Those two bastards would likely turn tail and run now, the only place two sniveling coward bastards were likely to go—behind a woman's skirts…or in this case, her family.

It wouldn't likely take him long to find out what he needed to know on the Internet. Morton smirked because his daddy didn't have any damn clue how to use a computer or the Internet. But Morton knew, he'd taught himself, and was pretty damn good at ferreting out information like where people lived.

So he'd take a look-see, and then he'd pack the rest of his C4 and his daddy's shotgun. Morton thought that maybe he wouldn't be coming back to this house. Maybe the C4 had a better use than what he originally thought. That would leave him with his daddy's twelve gauge, and against a woman, a twelve gauge was plenty.

He set to work at his computer, but the fact was, he knew quite a bit about the Benedicts already, as his daddy had once told him it would be a good family for him to marry into. He was glad now he hadn't.

Be kind of hard to take up arms against kin.

## Chapter 18

"One thing for certain, these weren't random acts," Caleb Benedict said. "No way in hell."

Susan noticed the sparkle in her father's eyes. Nothing Caleb Benedict liked better than a whiff of the job he'd loved for so many years. That had become especially apparent in the last little while. He'd perked right up a few months before when Kelsey had been in danger, relishing the opportunity to put his mind to work on the situation. She knew her cousin Adam would, from time to time, consult with Caleb—even, Susan suspected, when Adam didn't really need the help.

This time was different because now her men were in danger, and she wanted her father's help, desperately.

"This kind of targeted attack is personal," Jonathan, Susan's other father, said. "With you two men as the target."

They sat around the dining room table in the Big House, the homestead that Sarah Carmichael Benedict and her two husbands occupied in the late eighteen hundreds. This house had been the heart of the Benedict family from the very beginning of it. This dining room had been the heart of Susan's family all her life. Here is where they all came to get together for feasts, celebrations, and challenges.

"We've been trying to think who we've pissed off lately," Ryder said. "And all we've been drawing is a big blank."

"We just can't think of anyone who'd hate us enough to try and blow us up," Colt added.

Her men sat on either side of her, and Susan laid a hand each on their legs. Her mother had brought in some coffee and pastries earlier, and she, too, sat between her men.

Susan caught her mother's gaze and smiled at the acceptance she saw there. She wondered, then, if her men realized they'd already gained her parents' approval.

"The problem," Caleb said as he poured himself another cup of coffee, "is that you're equating these actions with logic and reason. Sometimes, those two faculties have no bearing on a criminal's actions."

"Personally, I'd say we're dealing with someone who's plum loco," Jonathan said. He looked at his brother. "Rigging a bomb to the front door of a house—anyone could have been hurt or killed. Letter carrier, salesman, hell, what if the Girl Scouts had been out yesterday? A sane person wants to kill someone, they aim directly at the target, don't they?"

"That's what I think, too," Caleb said.

"Oh, great. We have someone who's crazy after us." Ryder shook his head.

"We tried to think what's changed." Colt sat forward. He brought Susan's hand off his thigh, held it between both of his as he rested them on the table. "We thought that maybe the publicity around the deal we signed with y'all might have been the trigger." Then he met Susan's gaze. "Unless you have a couple of unhinged former lovers in your past, sweetheart. Because this is really the major thing that's changed for us. We found you."

"All of Susan's past boyfriends were heartbreakingly boring," Bernice Benedict said.

"Bernie!" Caleb looked shocked.

"Sweetheart!" Jonathan looked shocked and embarrassed.

"It's all right, dads. I *know* they were boring, and I know you all thought so, too." Susan threaded the fingers of her other hand through Ryder's. She liked feeling connected to both of them at the same time.

Colt smirked. Then he said, "Well, we're not boring, but we might be the opposite end of that spectrum—too dangerous to know."

"Don't you start that again," Susan said. She narrowed her eyes and pierced him with the hardest look she could muster. "If you think for one minute that I'm going to hide myself away while my men face danger, you've got another think coming."

Susan knew Colt had said that, thinking her fathers would step right up and agree with him. She knew that because the look on his face when her mother spoke up was a study in frustration.

"That's not the Benedict way, Colt." Bernice reached over and patted Colt's hand. "Though her fathers and I do appreciate your desire to keep her safe. You just have to find a way to do that while she's standing beside you."

"Hah," Ryder said. "No offense, Mrs. Benedict, but that would be easier to do if your daughter would just *listen*."

Caleb laughed. "Good luck with that one," he said.

"Could we please get back to the matter at hand?" Susan said. "You haven't told us what your contacts had to say, Dad, about the investigation in San Angelo."

"There was a great deal of hope when they recovered that one blasting cap. But when they checked the registration number, they discovered the damn thing had been reported stolen."

"Weren't they expecting that?" Colt asked.

"Well, yes, but it had been stolen about a decade ago. Reported missing in September of 2000. There'd been a few random thefts of caps and explosives in the Houston area, and those cases of theft had never been solved."

"A decade is a long time to wait for revenge, isn't it?" Ryder scratched his chin. "Hell, a decade ago, we were—" He stopped talking, and for a long moment, his expression said he was trying to reason something out.

Colt looked at him and slowly sat forward. "A decade ago, we were calling ourselves a couple of dumb asses because we'd been taken by Barnes and had to work long and hard to be able to start over again."

"Who's this Barnes?" Caleb sat straight and reached for the pen and pad of legal paper he had at his elbow.

"Morton Barnes. He threw in with us at the beginning, but then when the profits didn't roll in instantly, he pulled out," Colt said.

"Taking all our capital with him," Ryder added. "He made out all right, he must have gained a few thousand dollars for his trouble. We, however, were left holding the bag."

"Had to go work as roughnecks on a platform in the Gulf so we could get out of the hole that put us in." Colt ran a hand through his hair. "And didn't he start up a construction company right afterwards?"

"Damned if he didn't," Ryder said. "Though it didn't last long. I heard he wasn't doing too well, financially. That he'd been in some kind of brokerage business that became insolvent with the collapse a couple of years ago."

"I imagine if he ripped off a couple of men he'd partnered, he may have no qualms stealing some of the supplies he'd need for his construction company," Jonathan reasoned. "It's also not too big a stretch imagining someone like that, someone who'd suffered loss after loss, to work himself up when he sees the men he abandoned succeed where he can't."

"He was a mean little bastard," Colt said quietly. "Full of himself, too. The whole time he was in business with us, he looked down his nose at us. One of the reasons we didn't go after him when he ripped us off."

"Yeah," Ryder said. "We thought it worth the few grand to be rid of him. Even before he took off, we wished we'd never taken him on as a partner."

"Tell me all you know about this sucker," Caleb said. "And we'll see what we have."

* * * *

"You need to settle down some, son." Jonathan gave Ryder a level look then continued lighting his pipe.

They'd come out onto the veranda because Jonathan had said that was the only place Bernice allowed him to smoke his pipe.

Ryder rested against one of the pillars, folded his arms in front of his chest, and watched his woman's father. Correction, *one* of her fathers. The other one had grabbed hold of Colt, intent on showing him some of the historical artifacts the family kept in the library.

Ryder figured it was a case of divide and…what? Certainly not conquer. He might be off the mark, but he had the sense that Susan's family had not only accepted him and Colt in her life but approved of them.

Hell of a thing.

"I won't fully relax until Susan's back where I can see her. No offense to the security of your town, Mr. Benedict."

"Just Jonathan," the older man said. He sat back, and Ryder thought he wore quite the look of satisfaction as he drew on his pipe.

"Jonathan, then," Ryder conceded. And when Jonathan pointed to the chair next to him, Ryder figured he might as well sit. *Let the inquisition begin.*

"Bernice and Susan won't be gone that long. They just went to run a few errands, and besides, the entire town is on alert. Any strangers spotted will be reported to Matt and Adam."

Ryder exhaled heavily. He knew they couldn't keep their woman in their sight twenty-four seven. Hopefully, this worry would ease up once they caught Barnes—if, indeed, it was Barnes at the root of their troubles.

"Understand you fellas built yourselves quite a company starting from nothing."

"We've done all right for ourselves. We plan to do a whole lot better, too." Ryder stretched out in the chair, his booted feet crossed at the ankles. He folded his arms across his chest again, not as a sign of agitation, but because it was a comfortable way to sit. "But the truth is, we're just a couple of wildcatters at heart."

Jon made a sound that could have been a laugh or a cough, depending. "Hell, this family, this town, was begun by a couple of gunslingers who went and fell for a married woman." He took a moment to pull his pipe out of his mouth. "Being a couple of wildcatters who started out as two kids sleeping on the street and ended up savvy businessmen, hell, that's several steps up from that."

"Gunslingers?" Ryder had to admit he was curious about the Benedict clan. He'd heard a few stories down through the years. He hadn't heard about the gunslingers.

"The town trust established a museum a couple decades ago, smack-dab in the middle of Lusty. You should go over and have a look some day. But yeah, twin brothers Joshua and Caleb Benedict were hired to escort Sarah Carmichael Maddox from Chicago to here—where she was to join her bridegroom. Only, it turned out, her bridegroom had other plans for her than wedded bliss."

"So it started with them? Ménage marriages?"

"With them and their closest friends. Adam Kendall and Warren Jessop considered themselves a couple, and then they met Sarah's cousin Amanda. The two families—the Benedicts and the Jessop-Kendalls—decided to make themselves a town where people could live however they chose and be among friends." Jonathan sat back.

"And they called it Lusty," Ryder concluded. "Interesting name."

Jonathan chuckled. "Yep. And their descendants have been doing their best to live up to that name ever since."

"Apparently." Ryder sat for a few moments, wondering what Jonathan wanted, why exactly he'd corralled him to come out here. But the older man stayed silent, and Ryder felt the weight of that silence. It dug at him with tiny talons that seemed to pierce unerringly at his conscience.

"I'm in love with your daughter." Ryder wondered if that wasn't the point of being out here with his woman's father. "Colt and I are both in love with her."

"I know. What I'm interested in is how you feel about the fact that Colt's in love with her, too."

Ryder met Jonathan's gaze. "I first met Colt when I was eleven years old and I was being set on by two bullies." Ryder had never told this story to another person—not the whole of it, at any rate.

"These weren't schoolyard bullies. I'd spent precious little time in a school yard. These were teens. Hardened street thugs. The kind of street thug I was on the road to becoming, myself. At eleven, I was already running wild. Didn't pay to spend any time at home because my mother was usually hopped up on drugs and not alone. A couple of her men had thought I made a pretty good punching bag. One other thought I could serve a much more personal purpose. I got away from him, and that was the beginning of the end between Mom and me. "

Just thinking back to those early, nasty days made a terrible sweat break out on him. Ryder closed his eyes a moment, inhaled, and held close the reality of all that had come after that.

"Anyway, these thugs had me down on the ground and were pounding the shit out of me. Next thing I know, the one that was on top of me falls off me, unconscious. And there stood Colt. Christ, he was smaller than me, but meaner than a wild dog. He'd picked up a piece of pipe out of the alley and had whaled on the one kid. The other got scared and took off." Ryder blinked and focused on Jonathan. Susan's father just sat quiet, listening. "Colt and I have been together ever since, covering each other's backs. So how do I feel that this man who's closer to me than a brother loves the same woman I do? I feel right, and damned grateful."

Jonathan nodded, and Ryder had the sudden sense that he'd given the right answer. Then Jonathan took his pipe out of his mouth and knocked the tobacco out of it into a fancy looking pot beside his chair. "It's up to the men in the family to ensure their woman never feels torn, never has to worry about one being jealous of the other. Sometimes that's not easy, but it's always worth it." He pocketed his pipe. "Course, there's a huge advantage to sharing the job of man of the house. You're never alone when the tough times hit, and believe me, there will always be tough times. You have someone right there to share the burden of providing for and raising the family. You have another man that can understand you and your heart the way only another man can. And you have someone to help you keep a smile on your woman's face."

"If we have any doubts at all, Colt and I, it's about what kind of husbands and fathers we'll make. We didn't grow up with any kind of example of family."

"Having the example doesn't guarantee anything. Let me tell you, Caleb and I had the same concerns. You'll find out, it's both easier, and harder than anything you've ever done before."

"You can trace your heritage back generations. You need to know that neither of us can do that. Hell, we don't either of us know who our fathers were."

"I'd have thought with what you and Colt have built together on your own you'd have figured it out." Jonathan got to his feet.

Ryder also rose. The older man came up to him. His eyes crinkled, and his mouth tilted up in a smile.

"It's not the blood you were born with, or the heritage. It's not where you come from, son, and not the circumstances you're born into. It's what's inside you, and what you do with it that counts."

## Chapter 19

"It's never been like this for me," Susan said. Then she shrugged. "I guess I never really was in love before. But you knew that, didn't you, Mom?"

Her mother stopped beside her car and gave her a gentle smile. "That you weren't in love with those two you brought around last year? Yes, I knew. Mostly, I knew they weren't in love with you. It's all in the eyes."

"The eyes?" Susan opened the trunk of the car and set the two of the gallons of paint she'd just bought inside it. Her mother hefted the other two then stood back while Susan closed the trunk. Her house was soon going to be wearing smoke gray paint with burgundy trim.

"When a man's in love with you, all the way in love, you can see it in his eyes," Bernice Benedict said. "Those two men of yours look at you and it's as if you were the center of their world."

Susan liked that image a lot. "That's good, because they're certainly the center of mine. And it scares the hell out of me that someone wants to hurt them."

"I'm sure it does," Bernice said. "When you're in love, you become vulnerable in a very special way. Anything that threatens the men you love, threatens you."

Susan felt particularly blessed to have a mother she considered a friend. There'd never been anything she couldn't talk to her about.

"Did you have anything else you wanted to get while we're in town?" she asked her mother. They'd stopped at the pharmacy and the post office before coming to the hardware store to pick up Susan's paint.

It seemed like weeks, not days ago that she and Colt and Ryder had come into town and gone to Lusty Appetites, planning to get the paint after lunch. Fortunately, the man who ran the hardware store was a cousin and had kept the paint aside for her.

"Why don't we take the paint out to your house? I haven't seen it since you finished the kitchen. Besides, we don't get to spend as much time together as we used to."

Susan instinctively looked in the direction of the big house. She didn't like having her men out of sight, especially under the circumstances. She knew that wasn't logical, because there wasn't anything she could do to keep them safe beyond what they themselves were capable of doing. *No, not logical, but there it was.*

Aside from making a person vulnerable, love could also make a person crazy.

"Sweetheart, let your fathers have this chance to get to know your men. They're all perfectly safe, and I swear your fathers won't bite."

Susan grinned. "Yes, I know. I'm being silly. All right, then, let's head on over to my place."

The main street of Lusty, Texas, was a state road, and Susan's ranch—which was actually a corner of the original Benedict ranch—lay only a few minutes to the north.

"Winter weddings are always nice," Bernice said.

Susan split her attention between her driving and her mother. "I actually haven't given it much thought. A wedding, that is."

"You don't want to marry them? That doesn't sound like you."

Susan thought her mother was likely recalling all the times she had played "wedding" with her dolls. "Oh, I want to marry them."

"Oh, dear. You mean they don't want to marry you? Of course, they're not from around here. Maybe the notion of a lifetime commitment between the three of you is difficult for them to fathom."

"Mom!" Susan laughed. "That's not it, either. Really, we've not even discussed marriage. In fact, we really haven't talked about the future at all."

"Well, why not, for heaven's sake? A blind person could see you're in love with each other! You may think that kind of love is easy to find, and I can see how you would, considering all the examples you have of it in the family. But really, darling, it's not."

Susan put her turn signal on and then turned onto her road. Once she had the car straightened out, she shot a glance at her mother.

Every once in a while, she felt awed when she looked at Bernice White Benedict. Her mother was still beautiful in her mid-sixties, with very little gray hair and almost no wrinkles. She'd never known her mother to be unhappy, or worried, for more than a few moments in time.

Most of the women in her family could best be characterized as contented. She thought the reality of loving, and being loved by, more than one man was likely responsible for that.

"Well," Susan returned her attention back to their conversation, "if I had to pinpoint one reason we've all been silent on this particular subject, I would have to say that reason lies with Colt and Ryder's inability to see their true worth." She looked over at her mother and then put her gaze back on the road. "They keep reminding me that they're just a couple of wildcatters." She grinned. "As if that was a bad thing." Her grin sobered. "The thing is, they weren't raised in a loving family like I was. I think they're maybe a bit scared that they won't know how to *be* in a family, with all that entails."

"You mean children."

"Yes." Susan felt her insides melt when she thought of having children with her men.

"I wouldn't worry too much about that." Her mother patted her knee. "If I know you, you'll bring them around. A spring wedding would be nice, too."

Susan laughed. One thing she could always count on in life was her mother's optimism.

She turned the car onto her lane. She always felt such a huge sense of satisfaction when her house came into view. True, it had only been her home for a few months, but this place, more than any she'd ever called her own, felt like home.

She'd worked hard whipping it into shape, using money she'd earned herself. Soon, she hoped to refurbish the small barn. Then she'd see about getting a few cows and raising horses.

"It's all ready to be painted, I see," her mother said.

Susan pulled her car to a stop in front of the house. "Yes." Thinking of that fact, she recalled the afternoon Colt and Ryder had asked her to come down the ladder and then spanked her. She felt her face color and hoped her mother didn't notice.

"I'm not going to ask you what you just thought about to make you blush," Bernice said. She shut the car door and walked to the back of the car.

"Good, because I'm not going to tell you." Yes, she could talk to her mother about anything, but there were some things she thought she'd just keep to herself.

Susan led the way into the house, setting her paint cans down beside the door.

"Oh, I love this hardwood. Is it the original?"

Susan beamed. "Can you imagine some idiot laid linoleum over top of it?" She led the way back toward the kitchen, admiring the freshly refurbished hardwood that went from the front door to the kitchen.

"It could very well be that linoleum protected the floor until you could come and rescue it. Oh, and I love the way those granite counters turned out!"

Susan shook her head at her mother's observation. She had to admit she hadn't thought of it that way.

"The granite was hugely expensive, but when I saw the counters Steven and Matt put in at the ranch house, I knew I had to have it."

"I've been thinking of asking your fathers to redo my kitchen," Bernice admitted. "Aside from the benefit of giving me a shiny new work area, it would keep them occupied for a while. I swear, this retirement—where they've both decided to help me with all I do—is proving to be a challenge for me."

"The dads need a hobby," Susan announced.

"Don't I know it," her mother agreed. "But I hate to suggest it to them. They're so darn proud of themselves for learning to be...well, to be *housewives*."

Susan laughed because her mother's choice of wording was perfect.

A knock sounded on the front door. Susan frowned because she wasn't expecting anyone and family usually just came right in. Her mother raised her eyebrows, so Susan said, "Likely a salesman or a lost tourist."

She walked down the hall, thinking about just what sort of hobby her fathers could take up. She actually had an idea forming in the back of her mind but wanted to think about it more before she mentioned anything to her mother.

Susan opened the door wide and felt her smile fade.

The man standing on her stoop wore a beige Stetson, a tan western suit, and a neat bolo tie of dark brown. Behind him, gleaming in the sun, a shiny white Cadillac stood, driver's door open, engine still running. What snagged and held her attention, however, was the crazed, almost feverish, light in the man's eyes.

That and the twelve gauge shotgun he had pointed at her face.

\* \* \* \*

"Which of the two of you is the oldest?"

Colt raised one eyebrow. He wasn't sure what he'd expected when Caleb had ushered him off to the library, alone, to have a look at some family heirlooms. The question did surprise him, but there was no reason not to answer the man.

"Between Ryder and me? I'm four months older."

"Thought so. It's in the way the two of you react to each other." He said nothing more, just handed Colt what looked like a leather bound book.

"That's the journal of Joshua Benedict. It's a family tradition that the men in the family—or coming into the family—get to read that. His twin, Caleb—I'm named for him—wasn't much for sitting down and writing things out. That Caleb was the oldest, too, by minutes."

When Caleb said "coming into the family" it sounded to Colt as if he'd been asked his intentions. "I'm not sure I'm good enough for your daughter, Mr. Benedict. Or good enough to be a father. Bad blood."

Caleb raised one eyebrow. "Is that a fact? You think a man is limited to his antecedents? That just because your father lit out before you were born and your mother failed to do right by you, this cripples you?"

It was Colt's turn to raise his eyebrows. "You investigated me?"

"Hell, man, I'm a cop. You bet your ass I investigated the two of you. The moment my youngest son confessed what he and his brother had done. Damn fools, will they never understand women?"

Colt felt one corner of his mouth try to work its way into a smile. "Maybe you could tell me just what it was they did, sir. At the time, Ryder and I thought they…um…more or less gave us the green light to romance your daughter. If she was interested in us, of course. But now I'm not so sure."

"My younger sons are smart when it comes to business, but they have a lot to learn about women. Seems they pointed you both in her direction because you met what she'd confessed she wanted. Men made in the mold of her forebears, and like her fathers and uncles. Men unafraid to take charge. Josh and Alex thought she didn't know her own mind and had no idea what she was asking for would be like in reality. They thought she'd send you both packing."

"No wonder she was ticked at them," Colt said.

"Susie has a temper. I'm amazed she didn't have at them."

"Likely in deference to us. We were in San Angelo at the time."

Caleb took the journal back. "I recall one time, a few years back, running into Murph and having a drink with him. He told me then about his boys. I think you've both got what it takes to make a family—if that's what you want to do. It won't be easy, of course. But it'll be worth it," Caleb said.

"Susan's worth it." The words came because he wanted Caleb Benedict to know that.

The older man nodded. "The oldest becomes the legal husband. Then there's a family ceremony recognizing the three of you as mated. In Susan's eyes, and in the eyes of the family, you'll both be her husbands. If you decide to marry her."

Caleb led the way back into the dining room and left him with Ryder and Jonathan while he went to make fresh coffee. Colt looked at his watch. Susan and her mother had been gone for more than a half hour. He felt restless and edgy. *Likely because I'm not used to just sitting around and doing nothing.*

He pulled out his cell phone and called the hospital in San Angelo to check on Mike. Colt grinned as Nancy answered the man's phone and how, with Mike grumbling in the background, she complained about the old man's intractability and refusal to do as he was told. He wondered if that romance was fizzling out before it ever truly got started.

"How's Mike doing?" Caleb brought a fresh pot of coffee and set it on the table.

"Argumentative," Colt said.

Ryder laughed. "He must be feeling better."

"With that busted leg, he's going to have a few challenges when he gets out of the hospital," Caleb said. He nodded to his brother. "Jon got thrown from his horse once and ended up with a compound fracture."

"Don't remind me," Jonathan said. "They let me out of the hospital, but it was weeks before I could get around on my own. Wouldn't wish that on anyone."

"One of the things he was being argumentative about," Colt said, "was the suggestion that we hire a nurse for him. He says he doesn't need one, but honest to God, his house in El Paso isn't set up for a man in a wheelchair—which is what he's going to be for a few weeks once he's out of the hospital."

"I'll give him a call later," Caleb said. "Maybe he'd like to come and visit."

"We'd really appreciate that," Ryder said.

Colt looked at his watch. It had been forty-five minutes she'd been gone. "I don't care if she accuses me of worrying," Colt said. He punched in her number and listened to it ring. He counted them, and when he reached ten, he pulled back the phone to look at the display, checking that he dialed the right number. He had.

"No answer."

"Huh." Caleb reached into his pocket and pulled out his own cell phone. Colt figured he was calling his wife. The man didn't have to say he wasn't getting an answer. It was on his face.

"That's damned odd. Bernie always answers."

Colt had a very bad feeling in the pit of his stomach. He looked at Ryder, who nodded, indicating that he felt the same way. "Something's wrong."

"They only went to town," Caleb said. He dialed another number, and this one was answered right away.

"Matt? It's dad. Have a look around town for your mother and Susie, would you, please? They're not answering…they what? Okay, thanks." Caleb disconnected the call and frowned. "Matt says he saw them drive by about twenty-five minutes ago. He thought they were heading out to Susie's ranch."

That bad feeling turned into certain dread. "Aw, fuck." He didn't say another word, just rushed out of the house and headed for his Buick, Ryder by his side.

He had the key in the ignition before he realized that the Benedict men had gotten into the backseat.

"Seat belts," Colt snapped.

"Haul ass," Caleb replied.

## Chapter 20

Susan had one second to be scared out of her wits. Then she slammed the door, threw the deadbolt, and hit the floor.

A shotgun blast ate a chunk out of her door.

"Susan!"

Her mother's scream chilled her. She didn't want her coming out of the kitchen, down the hall. "Mom, get down!" Susan had rolled to the right of the door, toward her front hall closet. She ran the contents of the closet through her memory. Nothing in there to use as a weapon except an umbrella.

From outside, she heard the pumping of the shotgun. Her gaze flicked to the door, noting the hole in the middle of it, at about the same place her face would be if she stood next to it. Likely his next shot would be aimed at the doorknob.

"My God, Susan, what…" She looked down the hall and could see her mother huddling under the kitchen table, her head just visible. A quick glance assured her the back door was locked.

If that madman came around back, her mother would be a sitting duck.

"I think it's that bastard, Morton Barnes. Call for help!"

"Now you listen here, missy!" A disembodied voice yelled through the door. A second shotgun blast hit almost exactly where the first one had. "There's no reason to be calling me names!"

*No reason to call him names? Was he crazy?* "Are you crazy, you son of a bitch? You're shooting up my house!"

"You blame those no-account roughnecks you been keeping time with for that, missy!"

Susan heard another pump. She closed her eyes so she could envision the gun. That *had* been a twelve gauge, which meant likely a seven shot magazine. If he fired again, he'd have four shots left.

"Now, you send those bastards out here so they can face me like real men!" He fired again, and the hole was so big now that, if he wanted to, he could reach in and open the door—or reach in and kill her.

"No one's here but me and my mother, you crazy bastard!" She tried to remember everything she'd heard Colt and Ryder say about the man. A few details came to her. Mainly that he was arrogant and a snob. That and his last words told her what to say. "Pretty big man yourself shooting at two defenseless women, aren't you!"

Her thoughts raced. Where the hell did she put that handgun her father had given her last year for Christmas? She didn't use it often, but being a cop's daughter and a Texan, she sure as hell knew how to use it.

Could she kill a man?

Susan had never considered the possibility. The closest thing she'd come close to killing was that wild dog that had been rooting around back in her garbage last week. The damn thing had scared the shit out of her with all the noise it had made before she'd looked out the back door and seen it was just a dog.

And then she'd set the gun on the counter and made herself some tea. What had she done with it next? Taken it back upstairs? Or…

"I know them bastards are in there! Just like I know they've been sniffing 'round you so as to get that contract with your brothers. No other reason a company as big as Benedict Oil would take up with those two bastard no-accounts otherwise!"

"I told you, they're not here!"

Barnes' response was another shotgun blast, this one through the wall to the left of the door.

"Damn it to hell, will you stop trying to kill my house!"

"You watch your mouth, missy, or maybe I'll come in and kill you!"

Somehow, she thought that if he'd intended to do that, he would have done so already. He could have gotten into the house with his first shot if that had been his goal. Susan ran, crouched down, to the kitchen.

"Are you all right?" Bernice's voice shook, not from fear, Susan knew, but from anger. "I didn't want to yell out. I couldn't call for help. My cell phone is in my purse, which is in the car."

"So is mine. And the portable phone is upstairs. *Fuck.*"

"Susan! Such language!"

"Mom." Susan rolled her eyes at being chastised for profanity under the circumstance.

"What are we going to do?" Bernice asked.

Susan reached up and opened her junk drawer. She felt around and then cursed.

"What are you looking for?"

"My Glock."

"You keep your gun in the kitchen junk drawer?"

"Not always. I thought I might have put it there last week. But I guess I did put it away after all. Damn, damn, damn!"

"I'm gonna give you one minute to send those bastards out," Barnes shouted. "Then I'm coming in!"

"Susan! We have to do something. I'm not willing to just hide in here and get shot like some sniveling coward!"

"Neither am I." The only thing Susan could think of to use as a weapon was the shovel she had at the back door.

Another blast rocked the front of her house.

"Damn it, that's it! Mom, insult him!"

Susan stood up and ran over to the back door.

"What are you going to do?"

Susan didn't answer her. Instead, she said, "Mom, please, just do it!"

Susan opened the back door as quietly as she could and slipped out. Sure enough, her garden spade was leaning against the house, right where she'd left it. She hefted the long handled, round pointed tool and ran to the corner of the house. She peered quickly, saw Barnes wasn't in sight, and then ran toward the front corner of the house.

"You see here, Mr. Barnes!" Bernice's voice sounded strident from inside the house. "What kind of a Texan man are you, targeting women and children! Didn't your daddy raise you any better than that?"

Susan grinned. She guessed her mother thought that was a high insult.

"You leave my daddy out of this! You hear me?" One more shot blasted her house. Damn it, she was going to have to do major repairs. On the other hand, the asshole should only have one round left. And so far, she hadn't heard him pump the gun.

"Those bastards have got to be here! Damn it all to hell!"

"You watch your language, you poor excuse for a Texan man!"

*Go, Mom.* Susan stifled the urge to giggle as she reached the edge of the house and peered around it.

"I am too a Texan man! You got no call to say otherwise!" Then Morton Barnes began to mumble and pace back and forth between his Cadillac and the house. She couldn't make out what he was saying, but she thought he might have been talking to the car.

Then, from inside the house, "If you were my son, why, I'd scrub your mouth out with soap!"

*He's nuttier than a fruitcake.* Unfortunately, he was a fruitcake with a shotgun that had at least one more round waiting to be fired.

"Now, you see here!" He turned back toward the house and raised his gun.

A car horn blared from the end of the driveway at the same instant that Susan rounded the corner, shovel raised high, and screamed for all she was worth as she charged toward him.

\* \* \* \*

Colt's blood ran cold. He took in the scene in an instant—the white car and the man armed with a shotgun aimed directly at the house. He laid on the horn and nearly had a heart attack when he saw Susan tear around the corner of the house, shovel raised high over her head.

"Jesus Christ, woman!" Ryder shouted.

Morton didn't drop the shotgun, neither did he fire it. He saw Susan and began to run away from her, around the back of his car, then toward the front of it. But he didn't get into the vehicle. He just rounded the hood and seemed unable to decide if he was going to fire at the approaching car or the running woman.

Then he aimed the gun at Susan.

She'd followed Barnes around the rear of his car, but now, she hit the ground. Colt laid on the horn again, and Barnes swung the gun toward his Buick.

Susan rolled away from the Caddy. "Good girl." Colt slowed his car just enough, then rear-ended the Cadillac, stomped on the brake, and jammed the gear shift into park.

The Cadillac rocked forward toward Barnes, who screamed, backpedaling out of the way. He still held the gun but didn't raise it. Colt and Ryder had their doors open and were out of the car before it fully stopped. Ryder raced around the passenger side while Colt vaulted onto the trunk, ran up the car, over the roof, down the hood, and took a flying leap, feet first, kicking Morton Barnes in the head and shoulder.

Barnes crumpled in a heap on the ground, out cold.

The sound of a siren approached.

"I called Matt," Caleb said. Then he and Jonathan ran toward the house. "Bernie!" both men shouted at the same time.

Colt looked down to make sure that Barnes was out for the count. Ryder kicked the shotgun out of the man's reach.

"Thank God you got here. I was scared to death!" Susan ran up to him, and he scooped her into his arms, held her tight. His heart was pounding so hard in his chest he was amazed it didn't come right out of him. Then he set her on her feet and held her at arm's length.

"*You* were scared to death? God damn it, woman, the man had a shotgun and you were chasing him with a fucking shovel? *A fucking shovel?*" He shook her for good measure and didn't even care that her mother had come out of the house, flanked by her fathers, to witness his tirade.

The siren stopped as Matthew Benedict and a man Colt didn't know jumped out of the cruiser. Ryder stepped back from a still unconscious Barnes to come and stand beside Colt.

"I had to do something!" Susan stood toe to toe with him and shouted right back at him. God, he loved this woman. "That bastard was shooting up my house!" She pointed, and her next words came out almost as a whine. "Just look at all those holes!"

"Oh, right, smart move, woman. Much better he have a chance to put holes in you instead of your house!" Ryder yelled. "If you think the spanking we gave you for scaling that ladder to the roof was something, just you wait until we get you over our knees this time!"

"Don't you understand? You could have been killed. Then who the hell would Ryder and I marry?" Colt shook her again for good measure.

"You want to marry me?"

Susan's quiet question and her hopeful smile fizzled his anger, though he thought the fear would take a bit longer to go away.

Colt looked over at Ryder. "So much for setting the scene, pal," Ryder said.

He turned his attention back to their woman. "Yeah, we want to marry you. If you're willing to take on a couple of wildcatters."

She tilted her head to the side, and her smile widened. "If I say yes, does that get me out of the spanking you have planned?"

"No."

Colt grinned because he and Ryder said that at the same time.

"Good. Because, believe it or not, I want husbands who will look after me and give me hell when I do stupid things." She looked over at her brother, who'd handcuffed Barnes and, with the other uniformed man, was hauling the groggy bastard to his feet. "And coming after him with a shovel was stupid." Then she met Ryder's gaze, and then Colt's. "The answer is yes. Yes, I'll take you both on. And consider myself lucky to be able to do so."

Colt pulled her close, pulled her up, and laid his lips on hers. He sank into her, tasting her, claiming her. Then he eased back and passed her over to Ryder.

Colt smiled when Ryder kissed her, even as he knew that Susie got it wrong. He and Ryder were the lucky ones.

"Ahem."

Colt blinked and turned to take in Susan's parents and her brother, who were all smiling. The other man in uniform, Colt figured, was Lusty's sheriff.

"That was a hell of a proposal," the sheriff said. Then he shot Susan a level look. "That's one cousin I won't have to worry about anymore, I see."

Caleb Benedict came up to them and clapped both him and Ryder on the back. "I don't know what you two were worried about. Seems to me you know exactly how to be the husbands my daughter needs."

Colt felt the stress he'd been carrying slide right off him. He met Ryder's gaze and realized his best friend—his brother—felt the exact same way. They'd both been so terrified out of their wits by Susan's reckless courage, they'd proposed without any further self-doubts.

Of course, it wouldn't do to let their woman know that. Colt had a feeling that in the next fifty or sixty years he and Ryder were going to need every advantage they could get. Just as he knew they'd be blessed more than either of them had ever dreamed possible.

## Chapter 21

Susan Benedict loved family parties, especially if they were impromptu ones.

Her best friend and sister-in-law, Kelsey, had closed her restaurant to regular business in order to accommodate the flood of Benedicts, Kendalls, and Jessops who descended there on the heels of the arrest of Morton Barnes and hearing that she'd gotten engaged.

Even Adam, who'd driven the prisoner to Waco where he'd handed him over to the Texas Rangers, was able to join the party.

He pulled a chair up across from Susan, turned it around to straddle it, and reached for a handful of taco chips.

"That was some adventure you had yourself this afternoon, cousin," he said.

It had scared the hell out of her at the time, but already, the events seemed far away. Likely because she ended up engaged to be married to two of the manliest men she'd ever met.

"Very similar to the kind of adventure you had a few months back," Matthew said to Kelsey.

Kelsey shrugged, and then, because Matthew was still staring at her, she leaned over and kissed him.

"In hindsight, I suppose what I did was a little brash," Susan said.

"Only a *little* brash?" Ryder, sitting on her left, asked.

"You won't be saying that tomorrow, darling, when you can't sit down without a pillow." Colt, sitting on her right, said the words softly, but everyone at the table heard them.

The men in her family all seemed to take an interest in the chips and dip and peanuts on the table, proving they were smarter than the average male.

Kelsey sent her a sly grin, and she didn't need any help interpreting that.

Susan wasn't worried about the impending promised punishment. She recalled what had happened the last time her men saw fit to haul her over their knees. She'd discovered a heady new turn-on that day and was certainly looking forward to experiencing the thrill of that particular brand of arousal again.

The door opened to admit the rest of Susan's brothers. Alex and Josh each wore a worried expression until their gazes found Susan at the big round table. Susan wasn't surprised to see them, as news in the Benedict family tended to travel very fast. Steven came in behind her youngest brothers, carrying Benny Rose, the five-year-old son of Kelsey's newest waitress, Ginny.

Benny made a beeline for his mother, who'd just come away from the bar with a tray filled with drinks. Kelsey didn't serve alcohol in her restaurant, so everyone was indulging in iced tea and soda.

"Mom, I got an A!" Benny proudly held a paper high. Ginny set her tray down on the round table in front of Susan.

"Let me have a look at that! My, my, Benny Rose. Very well done!"

Susan noticed that Ginny's entire being lit up when her son was near. She knew the woman had been through hell. Now, she lived in Lusty, in Kelsey's former apartment, and had been taking counseling to improve her self-esteem.

Ginny proved her sensitivity to *Benny's* self-esteem by neither kissing nor hugging him. She offered him a high five, which the little boy gleefully jumped into.

"Now, why don't you run on into the kitchen. I'll be there in a bit."

Before Benny could move, Adam said, "Hey, Benny, can I see that A?"

"Sure thing, Adam. Look, it's the first one I ever got in spelling!"

As soon as Benny approached him, Adam put a hand on his back and looked over the paper. "That is very impressive. You must have worked very hard to get that A."

Benny's smile grew huge. So many of them had taken an interest in the little guy since the day he'd been left at Lusty Appetites. No doubt about it, Benny wallowed in so much adult attention and love.

"Nah," he stopped, looked at his mother, then said, "no, sir. Mrs. Parker is a really good teacher, on account of she makes learning fun, and my mom helped me study."

"Well, good for you. I'm proud of you, Benny."

Ginny picked up her tray and delivered the drinks to everyone at the table. Then she looked at Adam. "Would you like something to drink, Sheriff?"

"Adam," he corrected her gently. "I'll take a tea when you get a moment."

"I'll get it right away. Benny, you come on now, leave the sheriff be." Ginny nearly ran to get Adam's drink.

Everyone at the table saw the disappointment not only on Benny's face, but Adam's, too. Lusty's Sheriff sighed heavily. Benny obediently trudged off to the kitchen. Adam looked up at Matt. "I've noticed she doesn't call you *Deputy*," he said.

Susan nearly choked on her laughter, as did Kelsey. Adam wasn't the only male who seemed annoyed with them for that.

"What?" Adam asked.

Susan looked at Kelsey, who only shrugged. Perhaps another time, she wouldn't have said anything. But today, she'd not only taken on a crazed gunman armed with nothing more than a shovel, but the two men she loved had proposed to her—after a fashion. She could be generous to a clueless cousin.

She leaned over and said, "Adam, she doesn't call Matt deputy because she's not sweet on *him*."

She sat back just in time. Ginny came over with Adam's drink. Her hand seemed to tremble just slightly when she set it down in front of him. Susan noticed her cheeks had turned pink. Then she took off as if the devil himself chased her, disappearing behind the swinging doors to the kitchen.

"You've got it wrong. I make her nervous, is all. Damn it, it's been months since we fetched her from the truck stop and then charged that bastard Deke Walters. When is she going to stop shaking whenever she's near me?"

Susan looked at Kelsey and shrugged. She'd tried. Maybe things would be better if she just butted out and let things work out—or not—as they would.

Colt obviously decided to change the subject. "Were you able to find anything out about why Barnes came after us?" He leaned forward and put his hand on Susan's back. Because he'd asked what she'd wanted to, she looked to her cousin Adam and waited for his answer.

"Apparently, the downturn in the economy and his divorce pretty much wiped him out. He was overextended every-damn-where, and then a couple of weeks ago he received final notice of foreclosure on his generations-old family home. Funny," Adam shook his head, "though it's really not. All the way to Waco, he kept telling me what an important man his daddy was and how I was going to be sorry once his daddy got through with me."

"His father passed away shortly after our association ended," Ryder said.

"Yeah, so I found out. I think it more than likely that Mr. Barnes is headed for a lengthy stay in a mental institution."

"I don't care, as long as he stays away from what's ours," Colt said, an obvious reference to Susan.

Sandwiched between her men, with enough other testosterone makers around the table to give any woman a head rush, Susan didn't mind that declaration one bit. She felt the exact same way. As long as Barnes stayed away from what was hers—her men, her family, and her town—she'd be a happy woman.

* * * *

"Now, about that spanking."

They'd all just come upstairs after examining the damage Barnes had inflicted on her poor house. Susan turned around at Colt's words. He and Ryder stood side by side, stripped of their shirts, each wearing a determined look.

Oh, she was in for it, all right. She clenched her pussy, trying to contain her juices, and had to work hard at not smiling in anticipation. "Yes? What about that spanking?"

Ryder hooked his thumbs in the front of his jeans. "The way our kind of family is going to work is really simple." He paused for a moment to look at Colt. When he turned back to face her, she could see in his eyes the feelings he had for his best friend—his brother. "Colt's been looking after me, in his way, since that day so many years ago when he wailed on a couple of teenage punks who were beating the tar out of me. I can see no reason to change that now. As far as I'm concerned, he's the head of our family."

Ryder's declaration didn't surprise her. She'd known almost from the first that Ryder looked to Colt for leadership. She turned her attention to Colt. Someday, when the three of them were spending a lazy afternoon doing nothing, she'd tell them how special she believed they were, and had been, right from that time they'd traded untenable situations for the cold streets of El Paso when they'd been, really, only little boys.

"The days when you can act without thinking are over," Colt said. He took one step toward her. "My heart literally stopped when I saw you come around the corner of the house with that shovel raised, ready for battle. And while we salute your courage and we cherish *you*, sweetheart, we cannot let such reckless behavior go unpunished."

"You certainly got the thumbs-up for this punishment from every male member of my family," Susan observed dryly.

"Not *every* one," Ryder said, grinning. "I understand there are uncles and cousins we haven't even met yet."

Susan fought her smile. "Is this where I confess that any spanking you give me, no matter how hard, is just going to turn me on and get me horny as hell?"

"Oh, baby, we know that. If either of us thought for one moment you were frightened or hated it, we wouldn't do it." He smirked, looked at Ryder, then back at her. "In fact, I see our future, and what I see is you stepping out of line from time to time *just* so we will spank you."

Susan couldn't help it. She grinned. "As long as we all understand each other."

"I love you, Susan Benedict, and I'm going to gladly spend the rest of my life showing you." Colt's vow clenched her heart and brought tears to her eyes.

"I love you, Susan Benedict, with everything that's in me," Ryder said, "and I'm going to spend every day of the rest of my life giving thanks for you."

"Oh, God, I love you both so much." The emotion swirling through her nearly brought her to her knees. Never had she dreamed she could love so much.

Colt reached up and wiped the tear from her cheek. "Take your clothes off, woman. First, we're going to punish you, and then, we're going to show you your proper place."

The fine sheen of arrogance that coated Colt's words sent thrilling pleasure zinging through her. They loved her, they respected her, but in the bedroom, they demanded her obedience, just as here, in the bedroom, she needed to give it to them. Her fingers trembled as they worked to free her from her clothing. When she stood naked, Colt said, "Now, finish undressing us."

She began with Colt, acknowledging Ryder's assertion that he was the head of their family. She popped the snap on his jeans then pulled the zipper down, a task made more challenging by the fact his cock was hard, pressing tightly against the metal fastener.

She slid her hands into the waistband of his briefs, caressing him as she worked them to his hips, then pushed the clothing down. Slipping to her knees, she continued to work the clothing off, freeing one leg and then the other. She gave in to temptation and used her tongue to take a passing taste of his magnificent, erect cock.

"Vixen," he said.

Susan grinned then sighed. She turned her attention to Ryder and gave him the exact same attention she had Colt.

Colt stepped back then walked around to the side of the bed. "Come here. Lay yourself across my lap."

The tremor in his voice and the strength of his erection told her he was as aroused as she. Ryder offered her a hand, and she took it, rising to her feet. It took only a moment to do as she was told. The heat of his thighs under her hips and her belly seared her.

"We're each going to give you five good swats," Colt said. "Open your legs, Susan."

The moment she spread her legs, Colt's left hand splayed on her lower back while his right went between her legs, caressing back and forth across her slit.

She felt her juices seep out of her body and onto his fingers. His grunt of satisfaction struck a feral cord inside her. Without thought, she spread her legs even wider.

His first two smacks came without warning, hard and fast, and made her gasp. The sharp sting heated her ass. Like an electric current that heat pulsed out and down and in until it seemed to tickle her clit from inside her body.

"*Oh, God.*" She couldn't prevent her hips from rolling.

Colt's right hand, now warmer, returned to her pussy, this time opening her labia and gathering more of her moisture. "Mm, yes. You do like that. Your juices are nearly running out of you."

"Please, give me more."

"Don't worry, sweetheart. We will."

He suited actions to words, giving her three strong slaps that made her suck in her breath and blink away the sting of tears.

"Feel this."

Susan knew he spoke to Ryder and groaned when she felt a second hand caress her cunt.

"Nice and wet for us." He hunkered down and placed a kiss on her cheek. "I want Colt to finger-fuck you while I spank you. Let's see if you can come that way."

Ryder stroked her clit while Colt inserted two fingers into her. He spread them slightly and began to move them in and out of her. The combination of the two caresses shot her arousal to the very edge of climax.

And then Ryder began to slap her ass with a measured, strong rhythm.

"Oh!" Rapture flooded her, a tidal wave of ecstasy so strong she could only feel, only shiver and quiver, as pulse after passionate pulse battered her.

"Jesus, woman." Ryder's voice shook, and she knew just pleasuring her had brought him to the very edge as well.

It was the best orgasm she'd ever had, yet her elemental hunger for these men remained unabated. "Please, I need you both inside me. I need your cocks in me, please." She would have thought she'd been teased, held on the edge just shy of bliss by the way her body trembled for them.

"Yes, Susan, we're both going to fuck you now," Colt said.

Ryder lifted her off Colt's lap and kissed her. Hot, wet, and over way too soon, he used his mouth to let her know he would devour her if he could. Then he handed her over to Colt.

Her men wasted no time. They were all three past the point where finesse could be used. Raw, biting need nipped at them all, demanding hot, hard satisfaction.

Ryder moved quickly, grabbing two condoms out of the table by the bed. He laid one on the table and ripped open the other one, sliding it onto his rigid cock in one quick motion. He lay down on his back. "Give me your cunt, Susie. Take my cock inside you."

"Oh, yes."

Colt released her onto the bed, and Ryder took hold of her, bringing her over him so that she straddled his lap. Her right hand reached for his cock and centered it at her opening. Then she sank onto him, her eyes closing as the thrill and the pleasure of being filled nearly overwhelmed her.

"God, look how beautiful you are with me inside you," Ryder whispered.

His words melted her. "I love having you inside me. I feel so full."

"You're about to feel fuller," Colt said.

He got on the bed behind her, and the heat from his body covered her. She pushed her ass just a bit higher and nearly told him to hurry, but those words would have been redundant. He brushed lubricant over her anus then brought his latex-covered cock tight against her opening and began to push.

Susan sighed as she felt her anus open, as she felt him enter her. He used one strong, steady thrust to fill her completely.

"Fuck us, baby. Make us come."

Her hips moved in that unique rhythm, down and in and up and back, a sensuous movement of heart and instinct and need. Masculine hands anchored her, waist and hips, yet the control and the power was hers. Never had she felt so feminine, never had she felt so empowered as she did right then. The sounds of her lovers, sounds of growing arousal and nearing bliss, at once pleased and challenged her. She gave, and she gave, receiving back more than any woman had ever been given.

"Oh, yes, yes, you both feel so damn good, so close. Just a little—" The first contraction swept through her, an orgasm that consumed her entire being, heart and mind and body and soul. Pulsing strong, like the heartbeat of life itself, it came, and it came until she surrendered to it completely, until she collapsed on Ryder, their orgasms shivering and alive within her, joining hers, until she knew beyond doubt they really had been transformed from three into one.

Long, long moments later, when breath had been regained and condoms disposed of, the men came back to bed, one on each side of her. She lay on her back as they ranged above her, looking down at her. She reveled in the sensation of being cocooned in their heat and their love.

"Your mother told me winter weddings were nice," Colt said.

"Did she, now?" Susan heard the smile in her voice.

"Mm." Colt bent down and kissed her, his lips and tongue reverent in their caress.

When he pulled back, she turned to kiss Ryder. Each of her lovers tasted like more to her.

"We want you to have whatever kind of wedding you want," Ryder said. "As long as it's as soon as possible. We don't want to risk you changing your mind about us."

She reached up and stroked first Colt's face and then Ryder's. "You had it backwards all along, you know. I don't really believe that *I'm* worthy of the two of you. But now that I've tasted love under two wildcatters, I'm not letting you go, not either of you. You're good and stuck with me. Forever."

"Praise God," Colt said.

Susan knew, by the love in their eyes, he'd just spoken for them all.

# **THE END**

Siren Publishing, Inc.
www.SirenPublishing.com